Slashertorte: An Anthology of Cake Horror

Edited by Ben Walker

Table of Contents

This edition first published 2020 – also available as an ebook

© 2020 Sliced Up Press. Web: sliceduppress.com
Bluesky: sliceduppress.bsky.social

Special thanks to Steve Stred and Tabatha Wood

TRES LECHES

V. Castro

Tres Leches. A cake traditionally made from three milks. Evaporated, condensed and heavy cream. My recipe is slightly different as I make mine with the milk from the veins of my lovers, the ones who taste the best. Only high quality will do. One bite will leave your chin and lips a syrupy red mess as the sponge macerates in your mouth. The cake has a sexual fluids bitterness from my victims' arousal as they bleed, a copper tang that rushes down your throat in a rip tide of ecstasy. Wild with greed, you will be compelled to finish your portion then ask for more.

There are many ways you can make this cake. I like mine wet, sodden like my desire. Like the kind of sex that leaves you panting and weak on your back, your heart rate pulsating between your ears. The dizzying exertion worth the sensation that you may be on the brink of death. Every bite captures that experience. Leaves you satisfied to your marrow.

Three types of blood give the cake that lip-smacking flavor. First is the blood with the plasma removed, leaving a thick syrup. The second is the same as the first with a cup of sugar added. The third is blood mixed with liquid fat then whipped to merengue lightness. Tres sangres. A holy trinity of decadence for the blood drinkers and flesh flayers. Blasphemy never tasted so good.

The ground up bones of lovers who have hurt me or the bodies being disposed by the residents at The Pink Agave Motel a few blocks away act as the flour. The rest of the recipe follows the traditional method of the original tres leches cake including a simple whipped cream topping. Its blood-soaked richness hidden until you cut a slice.

My bakery, *Dark Delights*, is located in the Italian market in south Philadelphia. We are open on the weekends after midnight until sunrise. We keep a low profile with only bespoke orders. Word of mouth the only way to contact us. When you pass the small shop, you may think it is closed or abandoned with a faded red blind covering the window. In white, *Dark Delights* is printed on the glass with no opening hours. The door is locked at all times.

I miss my homeland; however, we have been here so long, I don't know when I will return. We lived through much tumult and war, moving around to avoid detection or capture. It has felt good to be in one place. As a high priestess, blood was my currency and my life until it became my lifeblood. The recipe dates back to after my days when I stood at the top of the great pyramids giving sacrifice to the gods for rain and bounty. When the Spanish arrived, I dressed as the warriors in head to toe cotton armour painted in the colors of the jaguar. We fought hard with axe and spear in hand. We cut down soldier and priest equally. Both vile threats to our way of life. Days and nights filled with ferocious cries under the scorching sun and rain to keep them from taking our land. But we had to retreat to the jungles to survive.

Hiding out and on the run left us hungry. That is when I had the idea. Nothing to eat but the bodies of our enemies.

Together we decided to make something sweet to cleanse the bitterness of our people's captivity and domination from our minds.

First, we bled the bodies. Then stripped their flesh to boil and roast. We left the bones to blanch and dry in the sun before grinding them between stones to create a flour like substance. Eggs from foraged nests. We built a pit similar to a grave and cooked it beneath the Earth as you might roast meat. It wasn't exactly a cake back then, but it satisfied. It gave us the strength to keep going. To hide and hope our people could survive. I prayed day and night to the gods to give me a way. And the gods answered. But not as I imagined.

They ambushed us in the night.

I lay bleeding, fearing, with a deep gash across my chest revealing bone and muscle. My heart slowed. Vision tunnelled as I watched the slaughter. The conquistadors shouting their language, my people shouting in ours. Both falling to the same oblivion. And isn't that the struggle we face still. The oblivion of mutual destruction. I longed for one last taste of something sweet to carry me to the afterlife.

I felt my arm being pulled above my head, away from the fight and back into the depths of the jungle. My body bumped and scraped the ground, but it was not painful because of the agony of my seeping wounds. A soldier flew through the air and fell without a head. I couldn't see who dragged me. The gods heard my cries. We stopped. Two women stood over me as I lay on the ground close to death. One looked as if her skin had iridescent scales, they shimmered like the inside of an oyster shell. Her mouth stained red. A creation from the Gods

I assumed. The other appeared human with obsidian blades for teeth. Could she be what the Spanish were calling a cucuy?

They looked at each other before taking a bloody heart from a leather that hung across the body of the scaled one. They bit each other's wrist before spilling their blood into the heart cavity. The reptilian woman kneeled and rested my head against her thighs. The woman with long brown hair kneeled next to me and placed the heart to my lips. It squished in my mouth, releasing its juice. It was sweet like my enemy cake. I sucked harder, my eyes growing. Muscles regained vigour as did my hunger. I ate until the heart was gone. I reached for the bladed mouth woman to kiss her deeply. Her mouth saturated with saliva and blood. The reptilian woman leaned from overhead and kissed me as well. Blood dripped from her chin onto my forehead.

"Rise, warrior priestess. We must flee."

We wandered as far north as we could, back then there were no borders with patrols. We just knew we needed to escape. Years passed with no invaders in that new land. Only the indigenous tribes who lived in peace with us, they knew we were different. Then settlers arrived on those shores. Again, we retreated until we learned to blend in. We took normal professions amongst the humans. It would be the only way to survive.

We three took up work at an inn for weary travellers, avoiding the human wars and helping when we could for those we deemed worthy. I found my passion again at the inn, baking human desserts. Learning their craft in the traditional way. When supplies ran low due to conflict, and we were left in need, my recipe came in handy again. This time I had space and time to perfect it. My companions chose the travellers they lured at the inn and their bodies given to me. Soon, the creatures living in the margins from all corners came passing through for the dark delights made in my small kitchen. All that time passed. I am still here enjoying, craving and creating Dark Delights.

CANDY BOY

E. Seneca

"Go ahead," he says. "It won't hurt, I promise."

You swallow heavily and stare at him, able to smell the soap wafting off his clean, bare skin, and he's smiling invitingly from the bed, one hand proffered. With trembling fingers, you take it, grip it tight; bring it to your lips and kiss his knuckles, and then you put his thumb in your mouth and bite.

There's resistance, just like you knew there it would be, and then his skin breaks with a splintering crunch and sweetness floods your taste buds. His severed extremity melts on your tongue, and just like he said, it tastes like cookie: a macaron, light and soft, and where there ought to be blood pouring out of his hand, there's only fluffy, pink cream. Your eyes dart up to his face, but he's smiling. "See? So go ahead. You can eat your fill."

You lick your lips, a hunger igniting in your belly, and you suck the cream out of his hand, making him shiver, toes curling in delight. You suck and suck until his hand collapses like a fragile sculpture made of spun sugar, but he only laughs. "Don't worry, I can always make another one." With his remaining arm, he pats his stomach. "Come on, why don't you see what's in here? I bet it's even tastier."

"Wait."

You get up and retrieve a knife from the kitchen, a long, thin carving blade, and as you straddle him again, all you can think is that this feels like a murder scene—but he all he does is grin, like you can't kill him even if you try.

"Good idea; I like the way you think. Here!" He stretches his arms above his head, arching his spine so that his stomach pulls taut, and you press the blade to his sternum—and stop, unable to bring yourself to actually slice through. What are you doing? What's wrong with you; you're not supposed to eat your lover; what are you—a praying mantis, a spider?

His fingers wrap around your hand, and he holds your gaze with two shiny, candy-like eyes as he drags the blade down his chest all the way to his navel. Cream spills out over the split in his flesh, and he curls his fingers into one flap of skin and pulls it wide open, scooping up some of it and holding it up to your lips. Helplessly, you lick it up, and it tastes like strawberries. He's delicious, and you know he shouldn't be, and when you clean his hand, you nip off another finger, tasting chocolate where there should be bone.

"Look," he whispers, "isn't it pretty inside?"

It is. His beating heart is all striped like peppermint, his ribs clean and smooth like fondant, his stomach is bubblegum-pink like taffy; his intestines glitter like sugary icing, all of it bathed in cream. The knife is still in your hand—you could easily extract one piece or another, take your pick of the feast laid out before you. There's just so much to choose from. Can you really manage to eat it all? Does he really want you to eat it all? But looking at it now, it just all looks so *good*, and the sweet smell of fresh baking fills your mouth with saliva. You—you could it eat it all, you think. If you tried really hard.

He plunges his hand into his guts, swirling his fingers through the cream and scooping up what you think should be his liver, and it squishes softly in his palm like cheesecake. "Go on. No need to be shy. I wouldn't be offering if I didn't mean it."

It seems disrespectful not to at least *attempt* to eat all of him. Besides, he's so mouth-wateringly delicious, how could you not? Maybe—maybe you *can* fit all of him inside you, after all. You won't know unless you try. You press your mouth to the handful of what should be giblets but isn't, and you lick it up, tasting toffee mixed with the cream, little flecks that stick between your teeth.

"You're so good," you can't help but murmur, and think, distantly, the absurd thought that like this, you'll never have to buy sweets or make any ever again: all you have to do is pick up a knife, open him on the kitchen counter or the table, and feast your fill.

His eyes crinkle at the corners. "I'm glad you're enjoying it." He smears the rest in his hand over your lips, and while you lick it away, dives his hand back into his abdomen and withdraws another fistful of confection. What is this time? Is it changing? *Can* he change it? This time it's cookie, golden dough speckled with gooey, melted chocolate chips and drizzled in what seems to be vanilla ice cream, and when you eat it, your eyes slide half-shut and you groan in pleasure. You've never tasted anything more perfect—it's all exactly as it *should* taste, the divine ideal, the flavor and texture unattainable by any human baker. The vanilla is pure and crisp, the chocolate the exact amounts of sweet and bitter, each bite baked neither too much nor too little, just the right amount of crunch on the edges and softness inside.

He grins at your vocalization, excitedly reaching inside himself, groping and widening the long split down his front even further. "Here, put some of this on, it'll taste even better!"

That seems impossible, inconceivable; how can this get any better when it's already perfection? Then his fingers slide into your mouth, adding something that you think is marzipan. Whatever it is, he's right, unbelievably. Even more unbelievably, despite all that you've eaten, you don't feel sated at all yet. Surely you'll grow tired of so much sugar soon? Surely it'll make you sick?

But you're not feeling it: the only high you're getting is the usual pleasure of eating something sweet, and the pleasure of seeing him happy—he looks so giddy, so overjoyed that you're having a good time, and that makes you more determined than ever to finish as much of him as you can. If he's happy to be eaten, who are you to deny him that?

You eat, and eat, and eat. You tear off his glazed-sugar skin and he laughs; slurp up his fluffy, cream blood and he giggles; break his white chocolate ribs and suck out the syrupy marrow and he squirms. His lungs taste like crème brulee, and even though he shouldn't be able to breathe, let alone talk, he's still very obviously alive, his respiration rapid and elated. You still want to hear his voice, so you eat only the left one. In the process, you fully expose his heart, and there you stop, panting rather yourself, braced on your arms and leaning over his ruined candy body like an animal.

There's almost none of him left.

Only his spine, his clavicle, the back layer of his skin. One arm, and his head and neck. His heart, pumping away happily; his brain, his teeth, his sparkling eyes. You want to taste it all, and you don't yet feel full. If anything, you feel even hungrier than before. You swallow hard, tasting sweetness at the back of your throat, the sheer ecstasy on his face spurring you on further.

He reaches up and plucks out one eye, severing it as easily as picking a flower. It gleams wetly in his mutilated palm, and you take it delicately with your lips. Liquid chocolate ganache floods your mouth when you bite into it, and as you chew, you thoughtfully watch the way his empty eye socket begins to collapse, and the way his silky hair falls over his forehead, shiny with a sheen of sweat.

"Think you can finish me off?" he whispers. He shivers a little, as if the pain is finally beginning to register. "There's not much now."

Even as he says it, you know with a certainty deep in your bones that you'll finish him off if it's the last thing you do. All rational thought is fleeing you, leaving behind only the savage desire to consume until there's nothing left.

Your teeth tear into his throat and crush his windpipe. There's little creamy blood left, most of it having spilled into the sheets long ago. His breaths slow as you reach his teeth and they crumble like sugar cubes; his hair dissolves like cotton candy. His heart tastes dark, bitter and dense, filled with broken nuts, and it pulses in your mouth as you chew. His skull cracks easily beneath your fingernail, and the treasure within is a layer of fondant covering moist marbled cake, glinting with flecks of cinnamon. The thought doesn't even cross your mind anymore that this is a human being, or once was. It's just a feast, just for you. You're not going to let it go to waste. You eat, and eat, with nary a pause.

The sole thing remaining is half his face, fixed in a frozen smile. His eyelid blinks sluggishly, then stops. For a moment you contemplate leaving it. He said that so long as there's a part of him left, he'll be fine. But it feels like abandoning the last bite of a feast, the final few crumbs, the last crust of bread: wrong, somehow shirking your duty. You pick him up, barely larger than your hand, and heft him in your palm. There's still room inside of you, as if a bottomless pit has opened in your stomach, to be filled only with him. The hunger will not be soothed by anything else.

You place the final sheaf on your tongue, and suck gently. His skin melts sweetly, his eyeball dissolving like a luscious bonbon. That's it, he's all gone.

You sigh and settle back against the pillows, closing your eyes as contentment thrums through you, a deep sense of satiation settling over you. The ravenous hunger is gone despite the lingering sweet smells, and sleep pulls at you. There's no reason to resist it.

***

You awaken to a sharp pain. Something pointed prods at your skin, and you reluctantly open your eyes. The soft light of dawn pours into the room through a gap in the curtains. Still, you're not entirely sure what's poking you, and you attempt to sit up, more asleep than not.

"Oh, you're awake," he says, bright and cheerful, and with a horrible jolt, the events of the previous night come rushing back. You snap your eyes open wide, and your vision is blurry—but despite it, you manage to make him out, standing by the foot of the bed. He's all in one piece, wearing a white shirt that seems painfully crisp in the early morning daylight, hale and hearty without so much as a scar as remainder. Something gleams and flashes in his hand, spinning around and around, and the splinter of light glinting off the edge makes you realize it's the knife you had last night.

Your blood runs cold, prickling in your veins as if filled with tiny crystals.

He smiles, stops twirling the knife. "Your turn now."

THE TEA PARTY

Stephanie Yu

Liyan Gee had, since second grade, insisted on being called Leah. Even entering junior high, she dreaded the first day of school when teachers would try to wrestle her name down with their tongues, stumbling over the foreignness of the sound. "It's Leah. Just call me Leah," she would say, reflexively. They always breathed a sigh of relief as they made the correction in their attendance books.

Unlike Leah, Alison Gibson had no need for false names. She was the most popular girl in the 6th grade. Girls coveted her like a shimmery dress in a catalog, and boys coveted her like she was the one modelling it. Because students were arranged alphabetically by last name, Leah was always seated next to Ali in class. It was by this happenstance that they had become friends. To be a cold moon in Ali's orbit was better than not being in it at all, and Leah often couldn't believe her good luck. They passed notes to each other in class constantly, even confessing shared crushes. Leah loved Bobby Prescott, who was on the soccer team and always wore Umbro shorts, whether or not he was going to practice after school. Much to her mother's dismay, she had begged for a pair of the same shorts at Christmas, even though she had never once touched a soccer ball.

Leah's infatuation persisted until it abruptly ended at the start of the spring semester. After P.E. one day, as they changed out of their gym clothes, Ali made an offhand remark, her voice as thick and languid as cough syrup, that Bobby had asked her to the semi-formal. Leah stared stonily as Ali lifted her shirt above her head. She caught the flash of Ali's fingers, dark lines of dirt framing the half moon of her fingernails, the only smear on her otherwise elegant hands.

"Stop staring," Ali snapped, once she had smoothed out her shirt.

Leah's gaze withered under the glare of Ali's large, bovine eyes, but her thoughts lingered on those dirty nails long after the school day was over, when she was at home in her bed, crossing out the *Leah Prescotts* she had written fifty times over in her diary. So many adored Ali, but it was Leah (and only Leah) who knew that under that blonde hair and golden exterior was a specific filthiness to Alison Gibson.

Ali loved the mud. When it rained, Leah retreated quickly for cover. But not Ali, who would stare into puddles, watching the bubbles form and the earthworms pool to the surface. Her favorite activity was making mud pies or "double chocolate cakes" as she liked to call them. She was especially fond of bringing her childhood tea set of pale blue porcelain to the woods behind her house to serve desserts from the earth.

Leah thought they were too old to still be having tea parties. And she suspected Ali knew to be embarrassed by such juvenilities. Ali made her swear many times over to secrecy, making her promise she wouldn't mention the make-believe cakes to anyone — even to Leah's parents, who didn't speak English and would have no concept of what chocolate cake was in any case. Leah dutifully kept her oath and every weekday, once they got dropped off at the bus stop but before they were expected home, the girls would trudge through the tangled woods behind Ali's house to a clearing where a little brook supplied the key ingredient to Ali's rich mud batters.

Ali's chocolate mud cakes were elaborate creations. Often two or three tiers of claylike soil, covered in an earthy fondant. She even managed to achieve a whipped consistency to the mud so as to resemble frosting, not unlike the buttercream that adorned the cake at her last birthday party. Ali would work the dirt into a furious lather, whipping air into it like she was whisking a meringue. The result, Leah could not deny, was rather convincing.

But something about the woods deeply unsettled Leah, the way the chittering bugs would sometimes cease altogether, as if a beast had suddenly thrown its long shadow over them. The thought of fungi casting miles of invisible cords under the soil, manifesting in circular blooms of white mold over the always-damp ground, made her uneasy. Not like Ali, who would make herself at home, knees planted deep in the mud. Her fears aside, Leah would always put on an eager mask and hold up her blue saucer to Ali whenever she carved into her final creation and asked "Did everyone save room for dessert?"

Truthfully, though, Ali's cakes disgusted her and Leah had, on more than one occasion, considered bringing this up. But she chose instead not to compromise the fragile symbiosis that wove them together: the pull of Ali's strange luminosity, the security of Leah's unwavering fealty.

One day, though, Ali got mad.

"You never stay to meet him."

"Who?" Leah asked.

"The man that comes to have cake," Ali answered.

"What man?"

"He comes sometimes after you leave and sits and loves eating my cake. He always asks for more. But I always make sure we save one piece for you. See, I'm a good friend."

Leah looked suspiciously at Ali, watching her pour some water from a petite blue teacup into a mound of dark sludge.

"What does he look like?"

Ali shrugged. Leah rolled her eyes. Ali was always terrible at answering questions.

"Is he tall?"

"Huge."

"Is he fat?"

"No."

"What do his eyes look like?"

"Yellow, like a lizard."

"What about his skin?"

"Spongy."

"What about his hands?"

Ali stopped her work for a moment, paused in thought. "They aren't really hands," she concluded, returning to her mud frosting. "More like rakes."

"Then how does he hold a fork to eat his cake?"

"He doesn't. He just shovels it into his mouth with his rake hands. He's always talking about how hungry he is."

"Is he nice to you?"

"Sure. Nice and polite. But he has a nasty mouth full of rotted teeth from eating too much cake."

Leah started to get up to leave. She felt suddenly ill. Ali had an overactive imagination. The cakes were evidence of that. But this all felt too much, even by her standards.

"Stay," Ali insisted.

"I really should go home, Ali."

With a start, Ali's hand shot up, squeezing so sharply into Leah's arm that her nails drew blood. Leah recoiled, grabbing at the tiny wounds. The shock of the pain sent her backwards, planting a foot into Ali's freshly frosted chocolate mud cake. When she looked up, she saw an almost imperceptible change on Ali's face. The same look she gave when she mentioned Bobby asking her to the dance. The look of small pleasure in causing her pain.

Ali stuck her hands back in the mud with a squelch, breaking the spell. "You're just jealous because he wants to talk to me and not you, just like with Bobby."

The words stung more than the reddening nail marks on her arm. Leah never knew Ali to understand their hierarchy. She felt plain in comparison to Ali's conventional beauty. Worse than plain, invisible. She hated the way she looked and often found herself in front of the bathroom mirror sucking in her cheeks, imagining her inky black hair turned blonde, taking her narrow lids between her fingers and cranking them wide, as if shocked awake by electricity. But always behind closed doors, always in secret, and certainly never in front of Ali.

Maybe if she had been older she would have been able to articulate venomous words to meet the sting of that moment. Instead, Leah turned and left Ali in the woods at work on a new double chocolate cake, the shadows beginning to frame her delicate face as the molten sun slipped under the horizon.

The next day, the seat next to Leah sat empty. The teacher left the attendance box next to Ali's name unchecked. Bobby

Prescott fiddled with a love note in the pocket of his shorts, never to be delivered.

When the police came upon the woods behind Ali's house, the clearing revealed a tableau framed by sinewy trees, a lone blue teacup cast onto the ground. Rows of earth dug up in even, parallel lines; evidence of hands trying to cling to the ground, or claws in search of prey. Dried blood that bore little distinction from dark soil. And, at the center, the perfect facsimile of a slice of chocolate cake on a periwinkle saucer, waiting to be eaten.

***

Three weeks after Ali vanished, Bobby Prescott got the nerve to ask Leah to the semi-formal. The boost to Leah's self-esteem would buoy her through the rest of junior high and beyond, to a chief position on the school yearbook, a prestigious university, and, eventually, a fast paced career in editorial fashion. When she returned to her school decades later for the reunion, with her now platinum hair cut in a severe bob, dark sunglasses, and her body enrobed in a cerulean crepe de chine jumpsuit, she paused at the guestbook for a moment before a blank by her own name that read "Alison Gibson."

For a disappearance with no body, there were no laws passed in Ali's name, no walks or memorial 5K runs. Ali's star had faded quickly once she was no longer around. But Leah still remembered her stomach dropping every time she and her mother would run into Ali's mom at the ShopRite, smelling of vodka, sticking her whole hand into a vat of mozzarella at the olive station. It was that same feeling that stirred at the pit of her stomach now as it dawned on her that the alumni committee had forgotten to take the dead girl off the list.

But the memory was fleeting. Leah focused instead on absorbing her former classmates' faces, which had either grown flaccid or too pinched. When Bobby Prescott saw her from across the room, he shouted "Leah? Leah Gee, oh my god, is that you? I barely recognized you!" He had grown a patchy brown beard to cover a chin that had no distinction from his neck. Leah excused herself to pop a Xanax in the bathroom.

She was relieved when the event was finally over. When she had left her home town after graduation for a career in the city, she had felt renewed, like a reptile shedding its skin. It was jarring to see all those faces again, morphed with time and age. She did not come back often to see her graying parents for that exact reason.

But on the occasions when Leah did return, she would often find herself in the woods in a small clearing by a brook, thinking of the long lost towheaded girl she once called friend. Were her bones now dissolved into the earth she had loved so much? Or was the man in the woods still coveting his May queen, fawning over her rosy cheeks, frozen forever in death?

Leah still felt a pang of jealousy being in her shadow. What made her so precious was being stolen away at the peak of her youth, rather than being left to rot, like Leah eventually would, no matter how many fillers she used to shore up her face.

Lost in these especially dark thoughts, Leah would sometimes press her manicured nails into the mud, taking satisfaction in the suction that pulled her down. There in the mud she would remain as she waited to catch a glimpse of brilliant yellow eyes, the scent of upturned loam, the call of her true name, and the cold grip of long rake-like fingers closing around her own. Coming, at long last, to claim her.

GRIND YOUR BONES

Douglas Ford

With the flu epidemic going, and me and Clemens reduced to hollow-cheeked waifs caring for sick parents, along came the lady known as Mama Baker. She gave us each a piece of the soft ginger bread she baked as her specialty, the most food we'd seen in days. "Don't just start eating it though," she told us. "Like goes the saying passed down by the older folks: to keep the evil away, you put bread under the pillows of children. So you do that—you each keep that bread under your pillow for three nights. One day each for the members of the Holy Trinity. You do that to help us keep the evil spirits away."

Then she left, moving on with her wagon to sell the rest of her sweet loaves in the town's thoroughfare.

We watched her go with hungry eyes, holding our bread with delicate care lest our clutching hands caused it to crumble to pieces.

Mother Baker had seen her share of evil events herself. Once she had a husband that people called Papa Baker, but he died before Clemens was even born. I told him how Mama Baker changed after that. "She seemed much smaller in those days. A tiny woman, not like the way she is now, less tall and round. Before he died, her husband, Papa Baker, he was big and fat."

"Did she eat him?" Clemens asked. I told him about the bakers as a bedtime story, and I could've embellished the details just to give him a thrill. I knew what frightened him. Like the part in *Jack and the Beanstalk* that gave him nightmares—how the giant wanted to grind Jack's bones to make his bread. That detail gave even me a shiver. But instead, I told him what I really suspected.

"You see the little black hairs that grow out of her chin and how big her arms look?"

He nodded.

"Well, I suspect that Papa Baker didn't really die. It was really Mama Baker who died, and the man for some reason wanted to take her place."

"Why would he do that?" Clemens asked. As an older sister, practically his mother now, I ought to have answers to such questions, but I didn't. Somehow, the idea of the ruse alone gave me chills. Did he miss his wife so much that he decided to become her? Take her place by dressing like her and acting like her, figuring nobody would notice, and if they did, they wouldn't say anything out of politeness? Or perhaps I just lacked the proper perspective, and as I wasted away everyone just looked bigger and fatter. I changed the subject to the dog that usually followed Mama Baker around.

"You see the way that animal nips at her heels and snaps at her fingers, growling at her like it's starving?"

In the dull glow of our room's oil lamp, Clemens nodded.

"Well, that dog used to wag its tail and lick her face all over. Now it acts like it hates her and follows her only because it's got no choice."

"I hate that dog. Looks like it's hungry, too."

I nodded. "Skin and bones. It hated Papa Baker, by the way. Now it hates Mama Baker. Now why would it change its attitude like that?"

"Maybe the man made it eat Mama Baker, and it hates him because of it," said Clemens.

We both felt a chill in the air and pulled our blankets closer to our faces. I didn't mean to tell him a scary story, but I went it did it all the same.

However, the day she gave us the ginger bread, no dog had followed. That night, we took the bread into our room uneaten, just the way she commanded us to do. From the other room came the sound of coughing. We knew what form the evil would take if it came into our house. Our parents would die. We knew we must not eat the bread in order to keep them alive.

"Where was the dog?" asked Clemens.

"No idea." Then I looked at the ginger bread in my hand and thought of the story about Jack and the giant. "Maybe she killed him and ground up his bones to make this."

I said this because of what we both wanted to do. We so badly wanted to cram the bread into our hungry mouths. Our stomachs growled like feral cats, having had nothing that day but the raw oats I'd served, half a bowl split between us. The bread looked so good. And yet we couldn't let the evil come inside.

"Put it under your pillow and go to sleep," I said. I did the same, and extinguished the lantern. Then I laid my head on the pillow and willed myself not to think of the bread.

Eventually, I fell into a dream of Mama Baker squeezing her fat body through our bedroom window, somehow tip-toeing past us without making the wooden floor creak. An odor of death followed her as she went through our door toward our parents' room, where they both lay dead. "These bones won't do," she whispered hoarsely as she held up my mother's thin arm. "They're too brittle. I need young bones to make the dough rise." Then she returned to our room where she began tugging at my skin, trying to tear it away from my bones.

That awoke me in a sweat, only I found Clemens doing the tugging.

"Samantha," he said in a whisper, "I did a bad thing."

"What now?"

He pointed toward his pillow.

"You ate your ginger bread," I said, "didn't you?"

In the light of the moon shining through our window, I saw him nod.

"But not only that," he said.

It took me a moment before I understood and felt around under my own pillow to confirm his meaning. My bread was gone.

"Oh, Clemens, not mine, too!"

His eyes gazed down at his feet like he meant to cry.

"Stop," I said, "it was just a stupid saying anyway. Just a superstitious belief. Of course she really meant for us to eat it. Go back to bed." I watched him crawl back under the covers.

"You feeling better now? Your stomach full?"

He nodded over the hem of his sheets. I started to lay my head back, but looked up when I felt a cold draught. I saw the window open, the curtain flapping in the night breeze. Hadn't I closed it? No matter. It helped air out the strong smell of sickness that emanated through the house. I closed my eyes and drifted away.

***

In the morning, I awoke to find Clemens' bed already empty, the sheets thrown about.

Thinking he'd got up before me to relive himself outside, I staggered forth to find him. First, I took a cautious glance into our parents' bedroom.

Two faces gazed back at me, mouths hanging open, eyes wide and glassy. They finally died at some point in the night. Just like in my dream.

The evil. Clemens let it in by eating the bread.

Stupid boy. With that decision, we'd become orphans. We might even get separated. Bad enough to lose parents—somehow the prospect of losing Clemens seemed even worse. I couldn't let that happen.

I looked through the house, worried that he'd seen the dead faces of our parents first and decided to run away without me.

Panicking, I ran outside, hoping I might find him wandering the perimeter. What I saw outside our open window stopped me cold.

Clemens' night shirt, covered in blood. I looked around, seeing just empty space about. Over a rise I saw a column of smoke, a sign that Mother Baker had already started her baking. Instead of running to her, I picked up the night-shirt, and something fell to the ground. I started to reach for it, but then pulled back.

I started screaming and don't remember how I managed to stop.

Clemens' bloody ear, all chewed up by something vicious and hungry.

They never found the rest of Clemens. Said a starving animal must've climbed through our window and dragged him out. I had heard no struggle, and I told them so, but the authorities took one look at me and cited my thin, hollow cheeks and my starved demeanor as a sign of lapsed senses. "You want for sleep," they said, and when they gave me a warm bed, I sure did just that. I slept like the dead.

In the morning, they awoke me and offered me breakfast.

A fresh-baked loaf of ginger bread brought by Mama Baker.

All for me.

Just me alone.

THE PERFECT BITE

Tiffany Michelle Brown

Helen stepped into $C_{12}H_{22}O_{11}$—*they had to be joking with that name*—and breathed in the scent of sugar.

The shop didn't look like any bakery Helen had visited before. She was used to the aesthetic currently in vogue in the San Diego culinary scene—exposed brick walls, neon signs flashing social media-worthy sayings, café style seating, and bright splashes of color.

$C_{12}H_{22}O_{11}$ looked more like a laboratory or hospital corridor. Stark white. Sterile. Shining metal tables and countertops. Obsessively clean.

They get points for committing to a theme. If nothing else, this place is an experience.

Her boots clicked over the white-tiled floor as she approached a sparkling display case. Inside, an array of cupcakes stood sentinel, encased in metallic silver wrappers and topped with uniform swirls of white buttercream.

Helen picked up a menu. It was white—of course—with three silver letters emblazoned on the front: *C.H.O.* Underneath, it read: *Engineering the perfect bite!*

"Welcome to C.H.O."

Helen looked up and tried her best not to gawk. The man on the other side of the counter wore a starched lab coat, latex gloves, and goggles.

They are really invested, aren't they?

"What can I get for you?" the man asked.

Even though she knew the shop's gimmick, Helen still squinted and tried to guess at flavors. The confections all looked exactly the same, like run-of-the-mill vanilla cupcakes, but it was a finely crafted façade. She knew the cupcakes were supposed to taste wildly different despite their uniform appearance.

Helen didn't want to know what kinds of chemicals the owners of C.H.O. used to *remove* the natural colors from their cupcakes.

C.H.O.'s other unique claim, according to the material Helen's editor had provided her for the assignment, was a top secret ingredient engineered by the owners. It was supposed to stimulate the pleasure centers of your brain, changing your sense of taste so that you experienced what they considered the perfect bite. In truth, it was probably a sprinkle of nutmeg or umami or some other pseudo-unique ingredient. As a food journalist, Helen had tasted it all—and she could easily sniff out a bogus marketing ploy.

"What flavors do you have?" Helen asked.

"We have six flavors available for our soft opening: Ethiopian fair trade coffee bean, white sangria, salted chocolate malt, key lime with mango curd, smoked peanut butter and toffee, and lemon-blueberry-caramel."

"I'll take one of each please. To go."

Helen watched the man behind the counter reach into the display case with a pair of tongs she imagined mad scientists would use to handle beakers. He placed each cake into a silver box.

"Is there a way to tell them apart?" she asked.

"The flavor is printed on the bottom of the wrapper. If you want to be adventurous, dig in. If you want to choose your flavor, pick them up and take a look."

"Clever," Helen said. She swiped her *San Diego Sentinel* company card and plucked the cake box off the counter.

"Enjoy your perfect bite!" the man called after her.

***

The cupcakes were a pleasant surprise. While they didn't provide the mind-altering experience Helen had expected after reading about "engineered taste buds" and "injecting science into baked goods," they were tasty. Balanced. The butter-to-sugar ratio in the buttercream was excellent. The flavors were strong, punchy, and very accurate.

Would Helen recommend C.H.O. to the foodie community in San Diego? Yes.

She cracked open a bottle of wine, hammered out an 800-word review on her laptop, and emailed it to her editor.

She'd only eaten a couple bites of each cake, the requisite amount to judge flavor, texture, and mouthfeel. Helen placed the remnants of the cakes in their silver box and the box in the fridge. She thoroughly rinsed the six separate forks she'd used, one for each flavor, and popped them in her dishwasher. She changed into her pyjamas and settled into bed with the remnants of the bottle of wine to watch a reality dating show.

Two episodes later, Helen could feel sugar swimming through her bloodstream. She felt like she should run a few laps around the block, put together a jigsaw puzzle, maybe reorganize her closet.

But it was late and sleep sounded far more tempting. Helen turned out the lights, snuggled under her comforter, and let the sugar dance in her stomach.

***

When she woke the next morning, Helen's throat was dry, her lips were chapped, and her stomach felt like an empty well. Hollow. Gaping.

Realization crashed over her. She'd eaten the cupcakes from C.H.O. and then neglected to fix herself anything else for dinner. Rookie mistake.

Helen rose to her feet, feeling brittle and weak. She glanced at the empty bottle on her nightstand. The cotton mouth had to be from the wine.

She needed to eat something. Preferably savory and greasy.

She shuffled into her kitchen, threw open her fridge, and groaned in disgust. Something smelled absolutely rank in there, like wet garbage on a hot summer day. She slammed the door shut and took a step back.

Helen mentally catalogued the contents of her fridge—a block of cheese, some Thai takeout, a loaf of bread, some cold-brew coffee, and the box of half-eaten cupcakes from C.H.O. Perhaps the takeout had gone bad?

She held her breath, flung open the fridge door, and reached for the Styrofoam. She set the container on her kitchen counter, steeled herself, and flicked it open.

But the hot garbage smell did not assault her nose. The noodles smelled spicy and comforting and vaguely sweet.

Helen's stomach grumbled as she placed the leftovers in the microwave. While they reheated, she conducted a sniff test on the cheese, the bread, and the coffee, which all smelled perfectly fine. The cupcakes, however—Helen's stomach clenched and heaved when she smelled them. Her eyes watered and she coughed, her body completely offended.

She picked up the box and sprinted out of her apartment. She chucked the cupcakes into the community dumpster and forced herself to only breathe through her mouth in little hissing bursts until she was back inside her apartment. Blessedly, her abode now smelled like a Thai bistro. Much better.

As Helen slurped up reheated drunken noodles, she emailed her editor, Anthony. She told him that yes, she'd sent in an article on that new cupcake place the night prior, but she thought it needed some editing. She kept it vague. Professional. She knew something was wrong with the cupcakes from C.H.O., but she couldn't articulate it quite yet. Helen needed to talk it out in person. Her article certainly couldn't go to press before then.

Anthony emailed her back almost immediately. They had an editorial meeting the next afternoon, so they'd discuss it then. Helen closed her laptop, satisfied.

She decided she needed a shower. As the water warmed, Helen stared at her naked body in the mirror. Was anything different about her? Had the cupcakes changed her in some way? She poked her stomach, gazed at her skin, listened for torrential rumblings.

But everything was quiet and normal. She thought about the cupcakes, both digesting in her gut and decomposing in the dumpster, and bit back the urge to retch.

***

An hour after she'd emerged from the shower, Helen was hungry again. Her stomach growled and twisted with impatience. She needed to eat, but nothing in her refrigerator seemed appealing.

Helen considered going to the gas station on the corner to pick up a bag of chips or pretzels, but she frowned at the thought. Those wouldn't do. She wanted something different.

Her thoughts drifted to the cupcakes from C.H.O. she'd tossed, and saliva coated her mouth. She started toward her front door. Her hand was on the doorknob when reason kicked in. The cupcakes were *in the dumpster* and something was very wrong with them, right? Why was she thinking about them?

Helen's stomach cried out, heavy with desire, and then her feet were moving.

Minutes later, she stood in front of the community dumpster, staring at buttercream streaked with used coffee grounds, dust, and banana peels. Everything in the dumpster smelled like sugar. Like caramel and cookies and cinnamon and custard. Helen swooned.

She scooped up a half-eaten cupcake and brought it to her lips. It tasted better the second time around, its exquisite flavors bursting on her tongue. This was it. This was what she needed.

Helen climbed into the dumpster and fed. She quickly devoured the remnants of the cupcakes from C.H.O., but afterward, she was still ravenous. She shovelled a fistful of garbage into her mouth and moaned with pleasure. Each bite grew sweeter and sweeter.

***

That night, Helen dreamed of a lab tech surgically preparing cupcakes. Angel food cake. Cardamom whipped cream. A filling that wriggled and squirmed.

The lab tech was placing maggots one by one into the cupcakes, their plump, wet bodies reflecting the light. Helen licked her lips and reached out for the cake, desperate for a bite.

She was in so deep, she didn't hear her phone ring in the morning.

Or the next day.

Or the next.

***

A rapping on Helen's door jolted her awake. The first thing she noticed was the sensation of lying in a pool of thick, viscous liquid. The alien sludge beneath her made it difficult to move. Her skin clung to her sheets as if she were enrobed in honey. She pulled at the material lazily, trying to free her body, but she was covered in too much muck.

The rapping came again. "Helen, are you in there? I came to check on you."

She recognized the voice, but her mind was foggy and she couldn't place it. She groaned in response—or at least she tried to. Helen felt a deep tear in her throat as her vocal chords struggled to function. It didn't hurt, but something wet slicked her insides and trickled into her belly.

"Helen, we're worried about you. No one's heard from you all week."

More knocking. She had to get up. If she didn't, that man—what's his name—would surely pound on her door all day.

Helen heaved her body to a sitting position, and her bed springs creaked.

"Helen!"

She gazed down at her skin, if you could call it skin any more. Everywhere she looked, Helen saw red and pink and white. Blistering, open sores covered her hands, her arms, her legs. She raised a hand to her neck and touched viscera.

The strangest thing was that she couldn't feel any of it. Hazy as she was, Helen recognized she should be in intense pain. She held her fingers in front of her eyes, studying the wounds that graced her hands, wondering if she was dreaming.

Then the hunger struck her full force. That deep crevasse within her belly, calling to be sated. Need rumbled through her.

"Helen, you're scaring me. Can you please open up?"

She started toward her door, her bedsheets finally sloughing off as they dragged and caught on the floor behind her. As she moved, she heard wet plops sound around her. Her stomach twisted, and her mouth watered.

Instinctively, Helen squatted, scooped up handfuls of slippery flesh and half-digested garbage, and shoved them in her mouth. She delighted as the flavors of chocolate, sweetened condensed milk, and gumdrops painted her taste buds.

A new strip of her skin wilted and smacked against the floor. Helen was still hungry and she considered grabbing another handful, but...

"Helen." The voice on the other side of her front door was desperate.

She sighed.

Helen ambled to the door and undid the deadbolt. She stood there expectantly, waiting for the handle to turn. The door swung open, and there he was—Aaron? Andy? She knew it started with an A...

"Jesus, Helen," she heard him say.

Helen heard a crash and a flutter. She looked down and saw soup spreading across the floor, the day's copy of the *San Diego Sentinel* quickly absorbing some of the liquid. She recognized her name in print on the pages, a photo she'd taken of a cupcake from C.H.O., and the headline she'd thought was so very clever when she'd created it: *Saccharine Science Abounds at C.H.O.*

The man collected Helen in his arms and began screaming something. Helen could feel the vibrations in his chest, but his words were garbled, like he was underwater. She nestled in the crook of his shoulder, her cheek pressed against his shirt. She'd grown woozy now, unable to hold her own weight. Hunger continued to rattle through her like a train.

An aroma sweeter than fresh-baked pain au chocolat wafted up to meet her nose. Helen's head lolled on her neck, and her gaze drifted down toward the inviting smell. The soft skin that had once stretched across Helen's torso was now home to a gaping, gushing hole. Masticated food, trash, and chunks of flesh oozed out of the cavity—and so did the mouthwatering aroma of bread and icing and crème caramel. Fresh saliva filled her mouth.

Helen's gaze remained transfixed on her brutalized stomach as the man laid her gently on the floor of her apartment. She registered his frantic cries for help and felt the vibrations of his hurried footsteps as he paced. Helen's vision began to blur. Her heart beat laboriously in her chest, each pulse a warning of finality.

She knew she was dying, knew that her body was giving out. But she wasn't ready yet. There was one final thing she had to do. She closed her eyes, trusting her sense of smell, knowing it would guide her.

With her remaining strength, Helen dipped her fingertips into the sweet-smelling pit of her stomach. She raised her hand to her lips, shoved the slippery morsels into her mouth, and let the delicate flavors play across her tongue—the ultimate combination of sweet, sour, salty, bitter, and umami.

Helen's last breath was a sigh of contentment. After fifteen years of tasting all the culinary world had to give, she'd finally found it—the perfect bite.

BLACK TEETH

Sam Richard

"I don't think I've ever had cake at a funeral," she says, through a mouthful of food. Her words move through me like I'm made of smoke and they're tangible parts of her; they disturb me at my core. I force a smile and come back from the void I was lingering in.

"My wife—sorry, my late wife, Sandy—loved cake," I reply softly before moving past her and pushing my way to the men's room. I can't shake the vision of smeared frosting on the strange woman's face or her black teeth.

I've only cried in bathrooms. This isn't intentional, I think it's truly the only time I feel comfortable. The idea of bawling in front of two-hundred people makes me feel sicker to my stomach than I already am. It's like a brick lodged in my gut, I feel weighed down. I feel broken. And I am.

After the tears run themselves dry and my eyes are burnt out, I head back into the brewery. Everyone's talking loudly and I just want to crawl into the earth forever. Some people are laughing, others are crying, but most have a look of shock carved onto their faces. It's the same carving I recognize on my own face when I spot it in a mirror or shimmering window. I force myself to breathe as panic tries to rise in my chest.

Moving awkwardly through the crowd, I stop at the bar and get myself another pilsner. They know who I am and don't charge me, which is nice but also awful. It feels good to be 'known,' to reap the benefits of that, but my stomach hits my knees when I think about why I get free drinks. I imagine the brewery staff having their post-shift drinks, after we're all gone, and one of them somberly says, "To the widower..." and they all cheers. I don't think this will happen, but it would be nice.

I move past several groups of friends and family and find a vacant seat at the edge of the oval-shaped bar. As I lift my drink to my lips several people walk past me and all of them bump into my shoulder. My cold beer jostles on my face and streams down my beard, onto my tie and suit coat. The same suit coat I wore to our wedding, which is oddly fitting and harrowingly sad if I think about it for too long. I remember how good Sandy looked in her dress; how good she looked all the time. I get lost in her smile in my mind and find myself smiling for a moment before I remember that she isn't here any more. She's dead.

None of the people who bumped into me stop to say anything or apologize. I don't recognize any of them so I wonder if people often crash a funerary celebration, but then I remember that there are people who I don't know in attendance, like her old co-workers, and I let it go as I pat myself dry.

I look for somewhere to toss the soiled napkins, not wanting to leave them on the bar, and I notice that someone has taken a seat next to me. Her black dress and tights combo remind me of something Sandy would have worn. Momentarily, my eyes stay fixed on her knees which aren't awkward in the same way Sandy's were; she called them 'knock-knees.'

"This cake, oh my god, this cake is so good!" she exclaims as I meet her gaze. It's the same woman from before. Her face is plastered in white frosting and dried out cake crumbs, her black teeth click as she talks. Our eyes lock.

"I've really never had a cake this goooood," she says, ecstatically, her eyelids flickering in delight.

I couldn't look away if I wanted to. Her eyes pull me from my void. Our pupils dilate in sync and, for a moment, I forget where I am. I forget why I'm here.

Across the brewery, someone drops a glass and the shattering echo shakes me from my daze and suddenly I'm sitting alone. Images flash through my mind: Sandy and I in my old apartment drinking beers and listening to The Stooges in my bed after our first time having sex, the rotting corpse of a barn owl in a sunny field, a murder-clown at a haunted house trying to nibble my ear, a trash sculpture of bloody wire hangers, all-encompassing darkness which gives way to the woman's face, covered in frosting and dried out cake; her rotten teeth.

Her eyes bore into mine and for a moment it feels important. I try to focus on it, to understand it, but a hand slaps my back, and someone asks, "How are you holding up?"

It's my friend, Kevin. He stands over me, a lanky and tree-like presence that radiates warmth and compassion. Before I can answer—before I can know if I can even answer—he sits down and clinks his half-empty glass against mine.

"I don't really know what to say...but this whole thing is fucked and we're all behind you..." he trails off before finishing his thought. I know they are. But it doesn't feel like it matters. I try to thank him, but I don't have anything to give, so we sit in the kind of silence that would be comfortable, generally, but is made strange by the context. It honestly feels nice.

Tears try their hardest to come, but I simply don't have any, so I slowly drink my warming beer. Kevin silently gets up and walks away and I feel abandoned in this room full of people who want to help me survive this. The catch-22 of being widowed is that the only person who could bring me any true comfort is the person who I can never see again. I ponder this with a detached view of my circumstances as Kevin returns to his seat, two fresh beers in his massive hands.

Passing one over to me, we clink our glasses again and I take a mighty swig. As the cold, crisp drink pours down my throat, I see an image of my late-wife's face in my mind. She's smiling with a mischievous grin and a twinkle in her eyes. I want to reach out, to hug her, but I know she's gone. I try to keep her face at the forefront of my thoughts, but it begins to distort and convulse.

I see her in the casket we lowered into the dirt mere hours prior, I imagine nature enacting its eternal plans. Her time-lapsed rot and decay play like a film in my brain that I can't turn it off. Before too long, all that's left is a greasy skeleton with empty sockets.

A few tears fall, but the dams never burst. My body trembles and quivers; I can't form words. Kevin and I continue to sit in silence, and I can't shake the image.

Her skeleton stares at me before it begins playing in reverse. Her muscles and skin slowly come back, the cycles of decay now occur backwards, but as her face returns to normal, everything is wrong. Sandy is no longer Sandy.

Pulsing eyes stare back at me as I see the woman's face, still covered in frosting and dried cake crumbs, still black toothed. I try to scream but nothing comes out, like the night terrors I had when I was a child. I'm frozen. And as quickly as she came, she is gone.

I steady myself, trying to make sense of this. I reason that it must be shock. It must be trauma. It must be my mind attempting to make sense of this fucking horrible situation. A haze of calm comes over me as I take a giant gulp of beer. Breathing in and out, I center myself.

Turning to Kevin, I am alone again. At some point during my brief PTSD episode, he must have gone to the bathroom or gotten up to get another beer. But looking around, I realize that I am completely alone. The brewery is empty, not only of friends and family, but of employees, too.

Sunlight is coming through the windows, but the old brick building is eerily dark and cold. A chill goes through me as I stand. Racked with fear, I head for the door, looking back occasionally for any movement, any people. None of this makes sense and I wonder if I've lost it.

Maybe her death was too much for me and I've gone completely off the deep end. Or, maybe I've died, perhaps a stroke. Maybe this is what it's like to be dead. And, if that's true, can I find her? Are we in the same place? Every ounce of me wants to see Sandy again, to hold her and kiss her and tell her that I love her and that I'll never let anything tear us apart. Every ounce of me wants that to be real.

But I know it isn't, because when I reach the door and touch the handle, I hear a voice from across the brewery. "You're not gonna have any of this cake?" The shrill question bounces around in the empty room, but it also echoes in my head.

I push the door as hard as I can, but it won't budge. And before I can run, she's right behind me, breathing down my neck. Her breath is sickly sweet like rot and I can feel bits of damp food splatter against my goosebumped skin as she speaks.

"This cake is so goooood, you really need to try it."

Her tone of voice informs me that this isn't a request. I turn to meet my fate and our eyes lock. Our pupils dilate in unison, throbbing together in an arhythmic cadence.

"You'll feel better once you have some…"

There's nothing I can do. I can't pull away. All I can see, all I know is her cake-smeared face, those sable fangs. Her mouth is coated in pasty white gunk and her nubbed teeth are black as coal. I brace myself, anticipating cake; anticipating whatever lies beyond.

But instead of giving me a plate, or raising a slice to my mouth, she brings her face closer to mine. A gesture of intimacy.

I gag from the sweet rot breath, but I can't break away, so our lips embrace, and I feel her pushing the sodden cake paste into my mouth.

It sits on my tongue for a moment, sweet and rich like it's made with goose eggs, honey, and hand-churned butter. I've never tasted anything so decadent in my life. She keeps pushing more and more down my throat.

The cake is transcendent.

Everything evaporates and I'm staring at a short, awkward man. His eyes look sunken in and aged. He is standing out of time, like he has been drained of all joy and love; of all reason to live. I look into his red eyes, but they're staring at nothing and nowhere. It's like he's lost in thought.

I don't know what to say to this stranger, because I don't know what's wrong with him. But I look around at all the other people, who are also sad, and I think we're at a funeral, though I'm not sure for who. I try to remember the last funeral I attended, but it's just out of reach; it hangs vaguely in my mind with no details, only shadows.

There's a sweet taste in my mouth and my teeth hurt, but it's so good and rich and delicious. It must be cake! It's definitely cake. I don't remember eating cake, but this is the best cake I've ever had. It's weird though. Do they normally serve cake at a funeral?

"I don't think I've ever had cake at a funeral," I say to the man.

THE CRUMB READER

Jackson Nash

Grandpa Noah Carter was in a jubilant mood as he waited for the birthday girl to arrive. He sucked on an unfiltered roll-up, chewing stray shreds of tobacco, savouring both the taste and the satisfying weight of responsibility on his shoulders. His father, known to everyone as Daddy Crumb, had passed just last year at the age of 98. As the eldest, now 75, he was about to become the crumb reader.

Standing at his window, wearing his favourite Iron Maiden t-shirt and a pink cardboard party hat with a tinsel plume, he watched a gaggle of family arriving. It was one of his daughters and her brood. The youngest of them was pulling a little red car along on a fraying string.

Anyone else watching them approach would see nothing unusual about the house, which looked like any other on an average council estate in the South East of England. Grandpa Carter took a sip of murky, sugary tea from a chipped Queen Elizabeth mug, and smiled. On the inside, things were rather different.

***

Lisa Carter showered off the remnants of glitter and cheap make-up from the night before, something muddy rinsing from her hair. The row of bar stamps she'd collected on her hands faded. The puke feeling rose, fell. There was no way she was making a chocolate cake, ritual or not. What kind of family wanted you to make your own 18th birthday cake? The ingredients her mum Shauna had left out the night before sat unused on the chipped kitchen counter. As Lisa had been constantly reminded, it was important the cake be a personal creation, so Shauna was at her brother's house, to be sure she wouldn't interrupt. Lisa had watched as her mum did the sign of the cross outside the house, once the right way up and once bottom heavy, before immediately calling her friends and beginning a typical night of teenage debauchery. And now she was hungover as fuck, cakeless and late for her own birthday party.

She found mismatched underwear, jeans, a screwed up neon orange t-shirt, threw it all on. She scooped up the cake ingredients her mum had left out into a carrier bag, ready to sling them into the dustbin on her way to buy a ready made cake from the supermarket down the road.

***

Lisa arrived at Grandpa Noah's with not one huge cake—which ritual decreed must be in layers and sections as per the diagram—but three small ones.

"What's this?" Shauna hissed at her, eyes wide.

"Chill mum," Lisa responded, "it's the same fucking cake we always have, I just did it in three, no big." She'd taken them home first, thrown out the boxes and arranged them on cake trays. Poking in a bent and dirty cat food fork here and there to make them look home made had given her great pleasure.

Grandpa Noah's house didn't give her any pleasure. It was creepy. For a start Daddy Crumb had died here after his illness, but it was more than that. Christ on the cross lived next to a large model fairy with big boobs, a sticker on its base proudly proclaiming that it was hand-painted. Boxes of pamphlets with frightening messages on them from all branches of belief sat stacked on coffee tables. Spiders roamed the undusted crevices of the room, which were most of them as Grandpa Noah also didn't care much for housework, probably just one small part of the reason his wife had taken off long ago. A poster of a pentagram hung next to one crammed full of information about The Illuminati. Another with the grey head of an alien completed the triptych. All manner of tarot decks gruesome and beautiful were scattered about like confetti. Pipes, bongs, and liquorice rolling papers were as common in Grandpa Noah's house as cross stitch platitudes were in the woolly nests of other people's grandparents.

But these things by themselves weren't what creeped Lisa out. It was the memory of Daddy Crumb reading tarot, tea leaves, and the crumbs, at the dining room table. It was the way he looked when he gave a reading which scared her. If it was just tarot that was fine, but when he read the crumbs his eyes appeared to belong to someone else. They seemed too round, the whites nearly gone like some demented farm animal.

Grandpa Noah cleared his throat to address the thirty or so guests who were crammed into his dining room and spilled out through the open doors onto the weedy back patio.

"This is all very unusual," he said directly to the cakes. His first reading and already it was a mess.

"It was too big to all go in the oven at once." This was her ready made lie.

"She's lying!" shouted out a ten year old cousin with dirty blonde hair and an obsessive desire to be right. "They sell those ones down the shops"

A disease of murmurs passed around.

"What's the big deal? You'll all get a piece, you can give me my stupid fucking dare," – more shocked grumblings and a few gasps – "and then we can all get drunk."

An 18th birthday in the Carter family followed a strict order. Initial awkward chit chat came first, then the group photo. The cake was cut by the eldest, and everyone had a piece, no matter how small. Once the birthday boy, girl, or person finished, the crumb reading happened. Just like the cake cutting this honour also fell to the eldest. The cake crumbs showed the divine image of the dare, performed for exactly three minutes, supposedly securing once more the safety of the family. When the dare was over the presents were given and life went on. This was the way it had been for as long as any of them could remember. The last 18th she'd been to they'd made her cousin Phil run all around the council estate naked. He did it, got his presents – and a caution from the police - and the adults talked happily about another few good years in the bag , nervously joking about not upsetting 'the old goat'.

Shauna came to her defence. "She's had a hard time what with her dad leaving, she didn't mean anything by it."

Grandpa Noah conferred with some of the older members of the family for a while before putting his hand up for silence.

"We will do the reading as usual, given the circumstances. But I can't help thinking of poor Nora." He paused for dramatic effect and there were a few groans and some laughs. "And this... well, it's far worse. I can only read what the crumbs tell me."

Nora's crime was apparently too much flour. Daddy Crumb had told the story of Nora many times to the little ones, but each time he did her dare was different. One time Nora had to sit in horse manure, another time she had been made to walk across hot coals, she had even been whipped nearly to death with the schoolmaster's cane in one of his stories but Shauna had scolded him for going too far. No one could ever get the real story of this hazy ancestor known as Nora out of him and Lisa decided it was the same brand of crap all old people tell their kids, just another version of Santa's naughty list.

Lisa rolled her eyes. "I'm divorcing myself from you lot after this, it's so embarrassing."

They gathered for the group photograph. No one smiled. Lisa stuck her middle finger up. The cake was cut and eaten around a few dry, forced conversations. Lisa thought she heard whispering but couldn't make it out. Whenever she caught someone's eye they suddenly spoke loudly about the weather or this week's TV. She ate slowly on purpose, dragging the whole thing out for as long as possible. They all smelt to her of desperation, reeked of it.

She made a show of pretending to fall over and dropping her plate as she handed it to Grandpa, snorting with laughter at her mother who looked like she might wet herself with fear.

"There's no logic in it, you all know that right? I can't see how-"

"-disgraceful!" interrupted Grandpa Noah. "Daddy Crumb told me to expect this sort of thing one day, but I never thought it would happen." Their belief was the sugar coated rock upon which they all lived, even the ones who said they didn't surely had the fear somewhere in their bones. It kept them together as a family when most of society seemed to throw away their kin the second they were old enough to leave. Grandpa shot Shauna a look and she pulled Lisa into the little kitchen.

"I wanted it to be a surprise, but we've got you a car you ungrateful little twat. All of us put money in, me, Uncle Allen, Grandpa, even Annabelle and you know what a tight cunt she is." There was an indignant *well I never!* from the dining room, and Shauna and Lisa couldn't help but soften and smile at each other.

"Just do whatever it is Grandpa tells you, three minutes and you can have the car. Then we can all laugh about the goat and you get to drive to college next year instead of getting on a bus with hundreds of smelly students. And say you're sorry to Grandpa."

Lisa felt ashamed. However silly it was, this was their own awkward family 'thing'. All families had one. None of them had much money and they'd managed to get her a car. She realised how lucky she was, even in a family of oddballs, to be loved. Maybe one day she'd be the one to tell the kids scary stories and make up silly birthday dares. And that didn't seem so bad, it would actually be kind of sweet.

They went back in and Lisa apologised, tried her best to look excited when Grandpa Noah gazed at the crumbs on her plate. He seemed to pretend to go into a trance but his eyes looked normal, not the way she remembered Daddy Crumb's eyes. He was just an old softy at heart, she knew that really.

"What do you see, Grandpa?" said the brat cousin with a tone of mock innocence.

"A red car. And Lisa's there."

Shauna smiled at Lisa and Lisa gave her a thumbs up.

"And there's a rope."

"World's Strongest Man!" shouted the child. "She's gonna pull the car!"

Everyone looked satisfied with this – Lisa would look a fool struggling and straining as the car sat motionless. They'd have excellent videos for social media.

"Let's take the car to the goat fields by Maldon and I'll explain." They all agreed to meet there within the hour.

"For God's sake," Lisa said under her breath when she spotted one of the little ones playing with a red car on a string. If that was what counted as divine inspiration then it was pretty sad, but she remembered what her mum had said and forced a smile onto her face.

"Let's go then," she said, speaking loudly this time with all the enthusiasm she could find. "I want my new car."

***

Daddy Crumb had reassured Grandpa Noah no one would argue, no matter what the dare. It was for the good of the family. This is what he told himself as he tied Lisa's feet and hands, as he attached the rope to the tow bar, as he shoved a gag in her mouth.

It was part of the ritual to sing happy birthday for the entire three minutes of the dare. Rearranging his party hat in the rear-view mirror, he had absolute faith that, when he started singing and pressed the accelerator, most of the family would sing along with him.

AN OLD FASHIONED TYPE OF GIRL

R.J. Joseph

Even though Mama had always told her to get to a man's heart through his stomach, it was Granny who taught her how to put that little something extra in to make sure they stuck around.

Charla stirred the batter carefully, mimicking the slow roll of a stand mixer. She had one of those fancy things, but she only used it on certain holidays or when she was pressed for time—never when she was baking her signature Forever Cake. She sighed. She'd made this same cake three different times the past six months. She wanted this to be the last time she made it as an unmarried woman.

Charla was born to be a wife. Mama and Granny had carefully trained her in all wifely duties, especially cooking, housekeeping, and carrying herself as a respectful lady at all times. Granny left most of the lady lessons to Mama because Granny was no lady and didn't think a woman had to do that "silly play acting" to get herself hitched. So Mama taught her how to apply make-up so artfully it didn't look like you had any on and how to speak and laugh demurely. She also taught Charla to have a general interest in most things but never too much knowledge about one thing, except making men happy.

Men loved that she took an interest in the things they liked but that she wasn't smarter than they were. Charla had learned at a young age that she actually was smarter than most of the men she met. She just never let them know that. They also loved her 1960s aesthetic. She always wore her hair in a simple and sleek style, reminiscent of Diana Ross' flipped bob from when she sang with The Supremes. Mama always said, "Fads are trite and they change so you need to be timeless." Charla never made drastic updates to her hairstyle and never wore trendy styles. Her beautician was in the old neighborhood, an elderly lady who declared she'd keel over and die at her hair station before she'd quit doing hair. Ms. Bessie understood that Charla was special and she kept her fittingly coiffed.

Charla never wore pants, only dresses. And always with pumps. Not the six inch styles that were in fashion, but the four inch ones that always made a soft and graceful line of the calves. She might have considered pants for when she had to do dirty, outside work, but men loved doing things for Charla. She had a lawn man who kept her yard beautiful, a mechanic who made sure she never had to even put air in her own tires, and a handyman that fixed everything he thought might break down before the next time he came over. But none of those men could marry her and Charla needed a husband.

So she dated. Not from online like other people did but very selectively. She only dated men she met at the supermarket or the bookstore. He got bonus points if he told her she was pretty, even if he compared her to Jackie O. She was more like Ann Lowe, thank you very much, who styled even the flawless Jackie O. Charla had farsighted, genius vision like Ms. Lowe and she used it all the time. The fast talkers who admired her small waist, big hips, and smooth, dark skin were usually after only one thing. And the one who married her could have that one thing. All the temporary fly by nights couldn't even consider sniffing it.

That's the most important part of what Granny taught her about cooking and courting: give them a food test before you tried to commit. She taught Charla how to put a little of herself into one specialty dish to present to a man she thought she might want to marry. How he reacted to that dish would tell the tale. All men wanted you to cook for them and pamper them but only the man made for you would get a particular twinkle in his eye as he ate what you prepared. He'd let you know he tasted the effort you put into the dish and he'd acknowledge that. Only then should Charla plan to be with her forever husband.

Most men failed the test. If a man stuck around long enough for the two month mark, Charla would invite him to her home for a meal. If he progressed past that, she invited him again the next week. Some of the men never made it past the first meal. They'd gobble her food down with poor manners and not offer any compliments beyond unbuckling their belts because they'd gorged themselves. They farted and belched. They tried to take off their clothes because they thought being inside her home meant she wanted to have sex with them. Those men had to make the quick exit. Others made it to the second week only to do something rude like, announce, "You'll make some lucky man a good wife." That meant he'd take all the benefits but never wife her. Or they simply collapsed at the table. That meant they weren't strong enough to even consider to become her husband.

Charla really hoped the man she was making the cake for was as special as she felt he was. She was an old fashioned type of girl but he made her feel supremely unladylike, in the most delicious and decadent ways. She rubbed her hand across her belly, gasping as her core contracted at her thoughts and touch. She slowly untucked her blouse from her skirt and pinched a generous amount of her waist flesh. The tissue came loose in her fingers. She winced. That part hurt just a tiny bit but it was worth it. She put it in the clay mortar Granny had gifted her with and ground the quickly drying flesh with the pestle. The colors and the odor never grew any less fascinating to her.

Granny made sure she understood how extraordinary the two of them were. Their bloodline provided them benefits that could come in handy. For Granny, the gift was that of sight. Granny always knew when things would happen. She even foretold her own death—that's why she started her lessons with Charla so early. Mama hadn't gotten any gift, so Granny had never told her about theirs. Charla's gift was the little something she always put into her Forever Cake. It hadn't steered her wrong yet.

A piercing mewl carried up from the basement and Charla furrowed her brow. She needed to feed the babies before her date arrived so they'd stay calm and quiet. She never introduced them to her dates. There was no point in that if the men wouldn't be sticking around to play Daddy. She took the mortar with her to the basement stairs.

"Mommy's here, sweetlings," she cooed as she opened the door. She stirred the contents in the bowl with her finger and then poured it into her palm. Soft tongues dipped into her hand. The one called Patrick slithered up closest to her and she stroked his knotted head. She'd really liked Patrick and she just knew two months ago that he was the one. He wasn't. One bite of her Forever Cake and his transformation was instantaneous. She'd cried over that one as she carried him down to the basement to place him with her other failed dates.

Fred growled in the corner furthest away from her. He'd been there the longest, the meanest and the most unfit to be her husband. His transformation had been slow and torturous. Even now, ten years later, he was still changing, his flesh bulging and oozing as it shifted. No wonder he had such a bad attitude. But he needed her to take care of him, now. All of them did. Her babies. They were her creations, of her flesh. Of her gift. She had to take care of them until they expired. When her husband came along, he wouldn't change like the others. He would be fortified by her Forever Cake, stronger and invincible. The joining of her ancient flesh and his would be exquisite, even before they commenced on their physical relationship. Then they'd be married so she could have help taking care of her progeny.

"Mommy has to get us a Daddy. Be sweet now, and hush up so we can talk." The mewling stopped and halted shuffling indicated her babies were going back down the stairs to do her bidding. Too bad they hadn't all been that sweet or obedient before they'd changed over.

When she arrived back in the kitchen, she pinched another section of dark brown flesh from her waist and began the work of grinding it up again. She poured it into the main mixing bowl and began the slow rolling mixing motions again. Charla carefully scraped the mix into the prepared pans. She placed the cake in the oven. It looked perfect. This man had to be the one. She didn't need any more babies.

Besides, who knew how much tinier her waist could get without her starting to look unnatural? People might get suspicious and think she was some kind of monster.

AUTHENTIC EXPERIENCE

Risa Wolf

We start before dawn, me and my little apprentice, her muddy green eyes gleaming as she watches me knead the dough. This bit is critical—if the dough isn't right, we won't succeed.

"See, Zenzi, it has to be sticky enough to clog your ears effectively, but not so much you can't remove it," I murmur, and stretch a ball of dough between my fingers to demonstrate. "Too much kneading and it will let the sound through."

"Yes, Frau Holda." She pulls off a lump for herself and sinks her knuckles in, sampling the texture, as I wash my hands. While Zenzi tests the dough I take out several kilograms of butter to soften, make sure I have enough Dutch cocoa, then measure out two lengths of fresh cheesecloth to take with us, the snick of the shears loud in the kitchen. I snap my fingers at Zenzi, and she nods, cutting four plugs of dough as I drape one of the lengths of cheesecloth over her shoulder. We each take two of the plugs and roll them into cylinders, then stuff them in our ears. I snap my fingers next to my head. Nothing. She mimics me, then nods. I smile in response, slide the rest of the dough into my apron pocket, then we both leave the bakery to walk to our destination.

***

Sunrise sifts a faint pink glow, like currant sugar, across the tips of the fir and maple trees. The street is quiet at this time of day, not even an early morning bicycler to interrupt us. I have Zenzi watch the road behind us, since the dough blocks noise and therefore we won't hear cars coming. In all things, I want my little apprentice to be as safe as possible.

We smell the river before we see it, the water masked behind the trees as we approach the store that sells my pastries. The store windows are dark, but I can still read the new sign: *Authentic Donauwelle Kuchen, on sale tomorrow.*

What a joy it was, to have them approach me with this proposal! I hadn't had a request for authentic Danube Wave cake in years.

Zenzi starts skipping towards the part of the river that is right by the store, but I wave my hands at her and gesture her further. We need to be away from buildings for this. My favorite hunting spot is another kilometer down the road, across a large field: a wide gently-curving swathe of the Danube where the rising sun sparkles along the rippling waves, beckoning the nixie with their music.

***

We crouch at the western bank of the Danube, the warm smell of wheat chaff and the faint stink of trucks from the highway in the distance wrestling in our nostrils. Zenzi shades her eyes from the sun as I wait, watching for the moment when the waves start to play with one another. It doesn't take long, the droplets glittering in the early morning mist. I whistle, two low long notes, and one higher trill. The surface of the river breaks, revealing two seahorse-like heads. They stare at us, then submerge back under the waves as a third head rises.

I have hunted most of my life, from when my mother taught me and her mother before then, but I still feel the tremble low in my gut at her beauty. She ascends from the river, water sluicing from the white shimmering thing that looks like her dress. Zenzi's jaw drops, and even without noise I can tell she is saying "She's so pretty."

She is. This gender of the species is visually stunning, even with the oily black-green hair and the hint of gills where the neck meets the shoulder. Her large round eyes are a sparkling gold, her oval face reminiscent of a Nazarene-era Madonna. As she opens her mouth, I surreptitiously test the plugs of dough. The nixie opens her arms to us as she sings, trying to charm us. My ears are empty of anything except my heartbeat, but I stand and walk towards the nixie. Zenzi startles and begins to follow me, so I stop her with a sharp gesture. This is the sensitive part, and she needs to watch.

I measure my pace, slow so slow, and focus on the nixie's mouth, those red lips, the sharp teeth. I concentrate on making my face go slack, mocking the appearance of a trance. The nixie's eyes crinkle as I come closer, her throat visibly vibrating with the spell of her voice, and she stretches those long fingers out to me, so close...

Before she can reach me, I whip the cheesecloth off my shoulder and wrap half of it around one of her wrists. I jerk her towards me, gripping her other wrist before she can lash me with those sharp claws of hers, then bind her wrists to her body with the rest of the cloth. The nixie is shorter than me, but she's incredibly strong and fights wildly. I can feel the shudder of her screams as I hold her, and I wave Zenzi over.

"Hold her." I exaggerate my mouth as I speak, knowing Zenzi can't hear me through the dough, and point at the nixie's arm. Zenzi grabs tight with both hands as I loop one arm around the nixie's throat and plunge the other hand into my apron. The dough is still the right stickiness, so I stuff it into the nixie's mouth as she gasps for breath. Zenzi has been prepared for this part, handing me her length of cheesecloth. I wind the cloth around the nixie's face and head to keep the dough in place, the layers of the netting rendering her features into irregular beige lumps. Nixie are shapeshifters, but something about not being able to sing or see keeps them in the form they use to charm, and this form is what makes real Donauwelle what it is.

***

Back at the bakery, I use kitchen twine to tie the writhing nixie to my metal kneading table, neck chest waist ankles, then Zenzi and I remove the dough plugs from our ears and start the mixers for the marble cake. The noise of the nixie's struggles is still clear, but if she screams or sings, we can't tell.

Zenzi follows the recipe for the chocolate and vanilla sponge cakes perfectly as I heat the ovens, decant the Morello cherries into a sieve, and grease the cake pans. Soon everything is ready, and I take out my tape measure and select my fillet blade from the knife rack as Zenzi settles on a stool.

"Once upon a time, the nixie hunted us for food and sport," I start. "They would take our young ones and hold them down

64

in the river until they drowned, then eat them raw." I lay the tape measure on the nixie's stomach. I can measure by sight, but Zenzi has not done this yet, and the curve of a living being takes some getting used to. I want to show her good practices.

"One year a harsh summer followed a harsh winter, and food was scarce. One of the townsfolk's daughters was by the river and managed to scream before she was charmed. They went with their hoes and pitchforks and killed the nixie before the child was fully drowned. Since the nixie ate us, we decided to see if we could eat them, and they were delicious."

I plunge the fillet knife into the nixie's belly, and she arches in pain, her keening whistling through her nose. Fuchsia blood wells up around the blade.

"You stab first, to get the strongest reaction before you cut. Once that's done, they don't move as much."

"But isn't that her dress?"

"That's a deception. It's a skin coloration trick. All of this is skin." I slide the knife partway out, then twist to get the blade between the subcutaneous layer and the muscle of the abdomen. "You want an unbroken slice of skin for the Donauwelle that is two centimeters smaller than the cake pan. The dermis melts and spreads, so you want to give it room."

I finish the cut, using my ring finger to round the corners, then repeat the process for the rest of the cakes, laying each section of skin aside. I look at Zenzi's face, simultaneously avid and appalled, and grin.

"Want to see the trick?"

She nods like a wobble doll. I flick a chunk of skin from the nixie's side onto the table, then grab a cherry from the sieve and offer it to her. "Squeeze the juice from the cherry onto that bit of skin."

She furrows her brow, then hops off the stool, takes the cherry, and digs her thumbnail into it. A vivid burgundy drop of juice wells up, then splats onto the skin. The chunk of skin squirms and spirals as the juice seeps in, and Zenzi squeaks in surprise.

"What does that?"

"It's the acid in the cherries. It makes something in the epidermis twist up. That's how we used to get the real waves - the cherries keep releasing juice as the cake bakes, so you get wonderful ripples and a pudding-like layer between the chocolate and the vanilla cake. This is also why you have to take them alive. Once they're dead, the skin won't do that anymore."

Zenzi nods. "What do you do with her afterward?"

"She has enough skin on her back side to do another set of cakes, but once that's done, I have a butcher friend. He'll make nixie schnitzel for me. Now." I place the fillet knife in a glass and pick up the skins. "Ready to bake your first real Donauwelle?"

***

While they're still warm, I choose a cake to be ours and cut a piece. We sit at the front window to share it. Zenzi widens her eyes in anticipation. "Thank you, Frau Holda," she whispers as she slices her fork through. I follow her lead with my own spoon. The ganache splits perfectly, buttercream glistening, vanilla, and chocolate marble cake perfectly moist. I delight as the tart cherries burst with juice under my teeth, then pause.

I hold my mouth still to savor the true experience of authentic Donauwelle cake: the salt-sweet of the nixie melding with the vanilla, chocolate, and cherry flavors, alongside the undulation of the epidermis in its last phase. I shiver in pleasure at the sensation, the death-rippling of nixie skin like waves lapping across my tongue.

LEGS OF THE DEAD

Liam Hogan

After two hundred years on ice, Frankenstein's Monster (or just 'Monster', for short) returned from the frozen arctic wastes. Retracing the steps he and his doomed creator had once danced, he wound up on the strangely altered outskirts of Geneva, where he set himself up as a pastry chef.

His mismatched hands were perhaps a little too large, a little too clumsy, for the delicate task. But he struggled on, driven by a dark impulse to create that even he didn't fully comprehend. If he had been capable of it, he would have put blood, sweat and tears into his bakes, such was his passion. As it was, each cake, each pastry, still managed to contain an unintended part of him. A few coarse flakes of shed skin, a short section of wiry sinew, a yellowed nail, easily mistaken for a toasted almond—until you bit into it, anyway.

People once assumed that Monster was a scientific creation. That it was Frankenstein's genius that had reanimated him, that kept him alive far beyond the normal span of man. From everything the few survivors in the dark days since the fall could gather, this was not the case. Victor Frankenstein was a lunatic, more likely to set fire to his test subjects than revivify them. A dabbler in alchemy, in the arcane, the abstruse, a seeker after the forbidden elixir of eternal life. What he achieved, he achieved by the most unlikely of accidents. Or perhaps it was due to the casual whim of eldritch forces far beyond his and our understanding.

What Monster achieved, he achieved because of what he was. Because of what he was composed of. Or decomposed of, strictly.

Each rotten morsel, each putrefying scrap of flesh, mysteriously imbued with diabolical and everlasting essence, in its turn brought Monster's inelegant tortes and lumpen kuchen to fiendish life.

And, whether by demonic irony or because they were driven by the same insatiable appetite that drove Monster, all of the pastries that were birthed from his gaping oven emerged ravenously hungry.

Just as Monster had once taken time to gain mastery over his patchwork body, so these cakes, quivering with need, took a while to be able to act upon their murderous impulses. In that while, (and perhaps because Monster had not taken into account two centuries of price inflation), his wares, ugly and misshapen though they might be, had flown from his trays almost as quickly as he baked them.

They spread through the more cost-conscious sections of the city, from lake shore to the parks and foothills of the surrounding mountains, slowly gathering strength and enough motor control to begin their awful reign of terror. Many were consumed before they could do any real harm. But not all. Not, in the end, *enough*.

***

A cremeschnitte, its over-thick layer of custard hiding an extra dollop of Monster pus, bided its time. Squirrelled away for a midnight feast by the teenage daughter of a tax accountant, it crept out in the dead of night. In the morning, there was no sign of the family pet, except for a torn collar and a few scraps of mangled fur. A faint, silvery trail from the fridge to the cat bed and a smudge of icing on the cat-flap were early warning signs that nobody paid any attention to at all.

The cremeschnitte, in search of seconds, was itself torn apart by squabbling rats, and the few remaining crumbs that were lit by the pale dawn were hoovered up by early-bird pigeons.

A heavy kirschenbrottorte made short work of Frau Lanz, a frail, elderly widow who had purchased the rustic, cherry-filled cake as a rare treat. She had barely sunk her fork into one stodgy corner, before it reared up, enraged and bleeding kirsch. "It's alive!" were Frau Lanz's final, smothered words, as the cake fitted itself over her mouth and nostrils, the fork in her liver-spotted hands jabbing as often into her face as into the treacherous torte. Weaker and weaker she stabbed until the fork fell from her limp hand with one last, mournful clatter.

And so it went on, each day a different recipe, each day a new victim. If Monster had made a gingerbread house, Hansel and Gretel would never have lasted long enough to trick the old, blind witch; who herself would have been consumed before the children ever set foot in the forest, scant competition for a house that bites back.

Without fingerprints, with no murder weapons, and with only creme patissiere as a common thread, authorities were unsure there was even a link between the rash of cake-connected corpses. What sort of a murderer covers their tracks with icing sugar? Or leaves curls of tempered chocolate as a crime-scene calling card?

***

But it was Monster's last attempted bake, the appropriately named totenbeinli, or 'legs of the dead', that caused mankind's downfall. Monster had slaved long and hard over the biscotti-like, nut-rich bars, so much so that, while he waited for them to cool before putting them in the window of his small bakery, he had taken a quick nap, sprawled out of sight between the ovens and his flour-dusted workbench.

The freshly twice-baked bars, stirred into life by a healthy dollop of Monster's drool, robust enough to drop unharmed to the tiled floor, quickly converged on the slumbering giant, a half-dozen at his patchwork head and the rest at his splayed arm. Did Monster's lack of nerve endings render him incapable of feeling them begin to feed? Or did he perhaps dream that their eager attentions were those of the partner he had been cruelly denied?

Whether they had already taken their fill or found the necrotic flesh too rich a meal, the totenbeinli stopped there.

On awakening, numb from the pain and staring at his mostly devoured hand, Monster was heartbroken once again. Not because he had been nibbled, but because the totenbeinli were gone. Rejected by his creator, and rejected by his creations... Little wonder he abandoned his bakery and fled back to the glacier from whence he had come.

He gave no further thought to his feral, ungrateful offspring. But the tough cookies proved not so easily digested as his other bakes. These biscuits had munched direct on the mother lobe, on the undiluted flesh of Monster himself. These supercharged pastries weren't going down without a fight. Anyone who made the mistake of trying to eat one, soon found they were being eaten themselves. From the *inside*. Lodging in the oesophagus, climbing back up the stricken victim's throat to ride the bucking bronco of the convulsing tongue, these were more *abuse,* than *amuse*-bouche.

And the eldritch power that drove the totenbeinli also brought their victims back to a semblance of life, sending them lurching on dead legs into kitchens in a race against time to create ever more tempting gateaux and biscuits and pretty little tarts before the one they had consumed burst savagely from their chests in an explosion of creme anglaise.

The reports were treated as a hoax. At first. Biscuits? Re-enacting a scene from *Alien*? Laughable! Until a live news anchor, having consumed the fatal snack in the green room shortly before going on air, expired rather messily, disagreeing with something that ate her.

By the time the military were sent in, it was already too late. Besides, an army, they say, marches on its stomach. And the totenbeinli and their kin, whether through native cunning or sheer luck, made use of that weakness. Soon, there were vast army kitchens overrun by brain-dead squaddies, whipping up traybakes of brownies and blood-filled doughnuts.

As preppers vanished into their underground bunkers, stopping briefly to throw out anything sweet, anything even vaguely cake like, an international think-tank convened an emergency session, looking desperately for a solution.

The greatest minds of a generation could only come up with a single suggestion. Not a solution, nor a plan, nor even a strategy. Merely who to ask for hopefully more useful advice.

And so a crack team of huntsmen, survival experts, and nutritionists set out in search of Frankenstein's Monster. Only Monster, they figured, could stop the zombie-cake apocalypse he had started.

It took the best part of a month, a month they could ill-afford, as the totenbeinli evolved into whatever the most tempting treat was in each country they invaded. From fondant fancies to fruit-filled strudels, from eclairs to pastel de nata, they quickly spread, crossing borders with the rapid ease of perishable goods, their victims lurching from wrecked cafe to smouldering concession, looking for something to wash down whatever it was that stuck in their throats.

At long last, the team tracked Monster to the arctic cave he had carved deep into the ice. An endangered species pleading for help to save the last of humanity before they went the way of the dodo and shoofly pie.

Monster stared at them, an eye missing, half his face gnawed down to the bone, the fingers on one hand nothing but nubs. The remaining muscles in his throat jerked and spasmed as he slowly, deliberately, gave the rag-tag remnant of civilisation his considered response.

"Let cake eat them," Monster said, turning his back on the world of patisserie and of man one last time.

TIERS

Belinda Ferguson

The bride chose vanilla Genoise sponge cake with raspberry cream filling, wrapped in marzipan and finished with a final layer of rolled fondant. It would be delicately decorated with pale champagne coloured string work lace and matching live roses. I chose the Quicksand variety, both for the name and for the creamy petals that grow a darker shade of pink toward the center, accented with baby's breath.

The layers of Genoise and a large bowl of raspberry cream cooled in the walk-in fridge as I created the *piece de resistance*. I kneaded the fresh marzipan in my hands, no gloves, I wanted to feel the soft, warm clay-like smoothness of the confection. To hell with the stained fingers and nail beds, I needed to connect with my art. This would be the very heart of the wedding cake. I added food coloring, counting carefully drop by drop. Pink: one for the Maiden, two for the Mother, three for the Crone. Yellow: one for Earth, two for Water, three for Air, four for Fire. I kneaded the marzipan again. Perhaps it should be a little darker. I repeated the drops and the counting again, and then a third time. I smiled as the marzipan blushed with the exact shade of peachy-pink newborn-baby skin. Perfect.

I tore a fist-sized piece off the batch and began moulding it in my hands. I whispered words to the ball of marzipan. Words of warning, words about precautions, words like 'unwanted' and 'accident' and 'unplanned'. Phrases sprung to my lips. As it took shape in my hands, I told the tiny form how it was such a small and insignificant thing upon which to base a marriage. I patted its emerging limbs with my fingers, gently admonishing it for even existing. I educated it about divorce, about custody, about court. I sang to it about a far worse fate, the hollow loneliness of a home bereft of love, a home without commitment. I filled the tiny shells of its ears with stories of the foster care system. I told it where I spent my childhood. I told it to go home. I told it to unmake itself. I told it not to be.

I nestled the tiny form into the raspberry cream filling of the middle tier of the cake. They always cut the middle tier. They do that so the happy couple won't have to lean over and ruin their posture for the picture. I surrounded the tightly curled limbs and rounded head with a puddle of seedless raspberry coulis, careful to avoid the little face with its pursed lips and sweetly closed but lashless eyes.

I paused for a moment to admire my work. I had done a good job on the face. I even gave it the tiny dent in the upper lip that my Granny Annie said was made when the Goddess shushed little girl babies, so they would keep Her secrets. I knew her secrets, of making and unmaking, of power and images, of exerting one's will. Granny Annie knew the secrets, until I took them from her, along with her last breath.

***

I covered the little creature with a bit more of the raspberry cream to make a level surface for the top layer of sponge cake. To tame the crumbs, I covered the tier with a thin layer of buttercream, salted with three of my own tears. Orphan's tears would have been better, but needs must. My parents are long dead, so my tears would do. I reached into the emptiness of my soul and squeezed out one tear of remembrance, one tear of loss, and finally after some strain, one tear of sorrow. I named each tear for an aspect of our Goddess. I carefully inserted the wooden dowels to stabilize the layers, taking care they did not damage the tiny figure inside. I silently gave credit to my Granny Annie. I thanked her for her teaching as I draped a thinly rolled layer of marzipan and smoothed it over the cake. I glanced out the window, no moon rode high in the cold starry sky. Tomorrow would be the new moon, an auspicious day for a wedding.

***

I arrive early to assemble the cake at the wedding venue. The huge pale grey room is decorated in a winter wonderland theme. Swags of tulle drape the ceiling and top the doorways. Thousands of cold white fairy lights shine in the branches of leafless trees painted white and sparkling with silver glitter. Silver, white, grey, all the colours of the moon. Good.

The wedding planner flits by to insist that I stay for the meal after I set up the cake. Normally I would refuse, even at the risk of seeming rude. I would usually tell them I have another delivery to make. I am so very busy. But today, I will stay. Yes, I will stay and choke down a lukewarm rubbery chicken dinner. I will see this through.

I am seated at the very back of the room, sharing a table with a few tragically single, distant cousins and some unruly preteens, along with the DJ. And, ironically, the wedding planner.

As half-finished plates are being cleared, a burst of applause erupts in the room, followed by the sound of knives clinking on wine glasses. My glass is empty. There is no free wine service at the kiddie table. Though a cash bar dominates the corner of the room, I will not make use of it. I do not dare exchange silver in this room tonight.

The master of ceremonies, who has clearly made good use of his wine glass already, slurs an announcement into the screechy mic. The bride and groom rise to cut the cake. Cellphones and cameras emerge from every pocket and purse to record the humiliation.

Such a strange ceremony: the couple cutting pieces of a beautifully decorated cake to smash into each other's mouths. Professionally made-up faces, expensive wedding dresses and rental tuxedos, all dripping with frosting while family and friends look on. It always feels like some peculiar combination of food fetish and voyeurism. Is this meant to bring the couple happiness? Plant a tree for them, tend it well to bring them stability; that makes sense. Give them silver, give them gold to bring them prosperity; that makes sense. Give them pomegranates to bring them many children. No. Don't bother, too late for that.

The bride and groom grab the ribbon bedecked knife and cake server, both made of silver, thank The Three. Gladly, there was no need for me to surreptitiously change them out for my own set. I would have hated to leave them behind.

The photographer cries out for the couple to hold on for a moment. She changes their positions and then checks the lighting one last time before giving them the go-ahead. The crowd is practically foaming at the mouth. My mouth is dry. Is it the food? Is it the lack of wine? Perhaps it's the anticipation.

I rise from my seat and sidle over to the wall, quietly slinking toward the front of the room. I whisper the secret words to escape notice as I slip into a vantage point slightly behind the cake table. In my mind's eye, I see the sharp icy sliver of the new moon riding high among the frozen stars.

The bride and groom awkwardly feign loving gazes at each other. For just a moment, I catch a flash of contempt in the groom's piggy little eyes. He resents this woman and her child. He won't stay. He won't raise the baby. He is not committed to this woman. He is only doing what he has been told is the 'right thing'. He's making an honest woman of her. While he makes a lie out of this marriage.

I hold my breath as the knife slices through the tier, exactly where I had showed the bride the special mark in the icing. I told her to cut there so she would miss the dowels that hold the cake tiers together. But her cut will perfectly bisect the tiny creature inside.

The knife emerges glistening red, and the bride's face momentarily freezes in shock. The room falls silent. The groom swipes the blade with a finger and licks it suggestively. "Raspberry!" he yells with a rakish grin. The silence is broken by a rush of laughter. The second cut makes a perfect wedge, and the groom plops it onto the waiting plate.

The bride stares down at the side of the slice, her mind trying to make sense of the form. She has seen that form recently. In the dim room, the fairy lights dazzle her eyes. She's not sure what she is seeing. No, it's nothing, just her imagination; a swirl of raspberry cream.

Then her mind latches onto the image, the image she had seen on the poster in the clinic. She had run away from the clinic with that image burned into her eyes and brain. She had cried in her car for hours before she finally went home and told him. He had insisted they would get married, and promised he would take care of her. Take care of everything. He hadn't actually asked. To avoid the consequences of drawing attention to his assumption, she had agreed. Good-bye career, hello motherhood, hello dutiful wife, hello abuse victim.

Tears blur her vision as she blinks at the cake. The groom wipes the cake server on the side of the slice and the image slips away. It's just her imagination. She's exhausted and hasn't eaten enough today. Nausea begins to rise and then a violent cramp strikes.

She cries out and clutches her belly. Until now, no one had noticed the slight bulge in her hastily altered wedding dress. A bright red flower blooms on the front panel of sequined lace and spreads down toward the hem of her gown. A second cry escapes her lips as her knees buckle. The groom stands frozen, clutching the cake server, and staring at his new wife as she slides to the floor in a pool of blood.

The stunned crowd doesn't even think to stop recording and put their cellphones to their proper use. So I step out through the servery to the kitchen door and dial 911. I look up at the sky to see a shred of black cloud as it slips across the silver blade of the new moon and is sliced in two.

It is done.

EATER OF UNIVERSES

Madison McSweeney

Sarah entered the 24-hour diner at the corner of Dunn and Morrisburg because she was lonely and wanted to be alone among people. It was that, the people-watching, she was most interested in; the cup of coffee was just the price of admission.

But it was the cake in the display case at the cash that caught her eye. It was uncut and perfectly round, its innards cloaked in a layer of dark brown, carefully smoothed chocolate frosting. It aroused a sense of calm in her; but also of celebration. Of purpose. It was overpriced, but Sarah was depressed and hadn't had baked goods in a while. And she was alone, in this diner, with no one to judge her but the waitress, who she would in all likelihood never see again.

The waitress served her a generous slice and Sarah beelined for a back booth by a window, where she could enjoy her indulgence far from prying eyes. She'd forgotten to order a coffee.

The old man who came in behind her may as well have been in black and white. He wore a grey newsboy cap and a rumpled overcoat, and his walk had a pained, shuffling look.

"That piece of cake has been waiting for you," he said, taking a seat across from her without enquiring.

Sarah looked at him sharply. Why did men always have to police what women eat?

Sensing misinterpretation, he clarified. "Do you know it's been sitting in that display case, on that very same tray, for thirty-five years?"

"Really?" she said, humouring him.

"So, you don't know," he said, his lips pursing. "Interesting. I should have suspected it would happen this way."

Sarah regarded him warily, scanning for subconscious signs of danger.

"Before you take a bite, I have to tell you something," the man announced, his eyes glinting inscrutably. She almost expected him to reveal a third eye or an extra hand. "A confession, if you will. It's only right."

"Shoot," she replied. *Then go, and let me eat my feelings in peace.*

He pointed towards the dark slice on the plate in front of her, lying on its side like a capsized ship. "Forty years ago, almost to the date, the Eater of Universes was imprisoned in an egg."

The man leaned forward. "Can you imagine – a being large enough to consume infinity, compressed into that small of a space?"

"No," she said. "I can't."

He leaned back, his left arm draped casually over the table, encroaching unpleasantly close to her side of it. "It was said that the touch of a woman's hands would free him. The woman who cracked the egg, we assumed."

He shook his head. "Of course, we had a vested interest in making sure he never got out, at least at first. Our Order was the one who imprisoned him, to stop him from devouring all the known worlds. And for five years, we served faithfully. But

I got greedy. Hungry. I started thinking, *Wouldn't it be a great thing if it were my wife who cracked the egg?*"

"I figured, if it *were* my wife, and she was the one who absorbed his powers, I would be able to control them. After all, I did a fine job controlling *her*." He blushed, suddenly remembering his listener's gender. "You're young," he explained. "That was what was expected of men in that era. And women expected it, too."

Sarah nodded, even though her stomach was in knots. She very much wanted this man to leave.

He removed his glasses self-consciously, not wanting to meet her eyes. "We all took guard duties of no more than a day or two, because we thought sustained contact for any longer than that would drive a human mad. When my night came around, I stole the egg, brought it home with me, and slipped it into one of the cartons in our fridge."

He smiled sadly. "My wife almost caught on. 'I was so sure we were down to six eggs,' she said to me. But I just chuckled and told her, 'Lucky number seven!'"

Sarah laughed lightly, thinking it was the reaction he was expecting. But he only stared back at her sternly.

"My wife baked a cake with those eggs," he continued, answering a question she had not asked. "And at first nothing happened. I lost faith, even as my wife left the cake near the window to cool. I thought maybe it had all been lies, that the Eater was not inside the cake, had not been inside the egg, maybe never existed outside of prophecy and the ravings of gifted lunatics."

"And then I heard a scream from the next room. I ran in, and my wife's hands were covered in blood."

Sarah froze. Her eyes flicked to the counter, but the waitress was somewhere in the back.

The man picked up a salt shaker and pounded the table with it, demanding more attention. "She had not been *cut*," he stressed, his voice tense and taut like a tripwire. "It was as if she'd dipped both hands in acid and the skin had dissolved right off."

"When I got back from the hospital, the cake wasn't on the counter. Gone. I was frantic. I knocked on every door of my block, demanding the neighbours tell me if they'd seen it." A wry smirk. "I must have appeared quite insane."

You don't say, Sarah thought, but said nothing.

"Eventually, I got the message. I'd overstepped, offended the Eater. Spit in his face, practically." He was polishing his glasses now, his movements quick and precise, his intense focus belying a muted hysteria that was overtaking him. "I was unworthy of him. The next day, I gave my resignation to the Order, in a letter. And then I decided to try to be worthy of my wife."

"I visited the hospital every day and sat by her bed until they kicked me out. She couldn't speak, and I couldn't hold her hand, but maybe just having me there..." He trailed off.

Sarah had been watching his fingers. When her eyes lifted, she saw tears pooling in the corners of his. *You're full of shit*, she thought, but the man clearly knew that.

"She passed three days later. The doctors never could figure out what was wrong with her. After they wheeled her body out of the room, under a sheet, I wandered here, to this diner." He rapped the table again, this time with just his knuckles. "I was completely numb. All I wanted was a black coffee, maybe some sympathetic conversation with a pretty waitress. But when I walked up to the counter, I saw the cake in the display case."

He paused to let the meaning of that sink in. "The exact same one my wife had baked just three days before, with the Eater of Universes mixed right in."

"Don't ask me how the cake got there, or why it chose to present itself to me right then. Cosmic joke, I think. And a sadistic one at that."

He pointed to Sarah's plate. "That cake, of which you have a slice in front of you right now, has sat in that display case for thirty-five years. No one has ever ordered it, and it's never been thrown out or replaced." He glanced at the waitress, who was busy mopping stains of cold coffee from a countertop, completely oblivious to the strange conversation occurring over her shoulder.

"I don't think the staff here even register its presence. It has that power - to only reveal itself to certain people. Others *see* it, but they don't think anything of it, or even remember it once they've looked away, if you know what I mean."

He pointed to one of the other booths. "A few years ago, I sat across from a young couple, like I'm sitting across from you right now, and, just to test my theory, I said to them, 'That cake up there looks delicious, eh?' They had no *idea* what I was talking about."

He looked Sarah deep in the eye, raising both of his brows, demanding a response from her. "Fascinating," she said, unsure what else was safe to say.

"Do you understand," he said, speaking more slowly, as if to an idiot, "that you are the first person in over thirty years to not only *notice* the cake, but to *order* it? Do you know what that means?"

"For sure," she said.

He didn't believe her, but stood up stiffly, gathering his hat in his hands. "I hope you'll give this some thought before you take a bite of that cake," he chastened. "Before you bring him inside you. Just know what you're getting into."

The door *ding*ed as the man stalked out. He tried to yank on the handle so it would slam shut behind him, but it wasn't that type of door.

The waitress perked up, startled. "Was he bothering you?"

Little late for that. "It's fine," Sarah said.

"He's a regular," the woman explained apologetically. "He's usually harmless." Her eyes flicked to Sarah's plate. "You haven't touched your cake!"

"Savouring it," Sarah replied, smiling tightly.

Sarah eyed the cake for irregularities, finding none. The slice looked moist enough; it certainly didn't appear to have been sitting out for over thirty years. She prodded it gently with her fork. She considered what it would be like to have the power to consume universes flowing through her, what it would taste like on her tongue. She mulled how stupid she would look if she walked out now, leaving her food untouched. She noticed how delicious it looked.

At last, she severed a chunk, deposited it into her mouth and swallowed.

As the Eater of Universes hatched inside of her, it felt like indigestion.

ONE YEAR ANNIVERSARY

Red Lagoe

If Gary could have devoured the remains of his bride without choking on the ashes, he would. The moment he held the urn in his hands he knew she'd never be close enough to him again. Even when he slept with the cold stainless steel urn against his chest, Kat was never really with him.

The sweet, warm aroma of her memory carried through the house as she expanded with the rising cake. Gary licked his lips at the thought of her joining him in a manner far more enjoyable than pouring ash upon his tongue. On the counter, the top layer of their wedding cake absorbed the radiant heat from the oven and thawed. Tomorrow, on their one-year anniversary, they were supposed to eat the saved portion of their cake. But her unexpected death left Gary to partake in the tradition alone.

When the timer sounded, he extracted the round pan of cake, risen into a mound at the center. The scent of Kat-infused chocolate was hard to resist. After it cooled, Gary frosted it with care, then placed the top tier of their saved wedding cake upon it.

Tomorrow, he would honor the ritual of eating the cake, and Kat would be with him forever.

***

Before dawn's light reached through the windows, Gary had already dressed. He put on his best suit and Kat's favorite tie and was ready to begin. He held a framed five by seven against his chest. A wedding photo of the cake-cutting ceremony. Instead of feeding each other romantically, they had smooshed cake in each other's faces. He recalled crumbles falling to the floor. Frosting smeared on Kat's chin and cheeks. Her smile through peach and pink frosting made him the happiest man alive back then.

Tears trickled down his cheek, hands trembled as he approached the kitchen. On the counter, where he had left the two-tiered cake overnight, the pan was empty. Spongy chocolate remnants covered the floor. Globs and smears of frosting of all different colors painted the tiles. He followed a trail of pastel frosting out of the kitchen and into the den.

In the pitch black reading room, where Kat used to sit reading her books late into the night, he flicked the switch. A soft yellow lamp by her favorite reading chair lit the room. Kat sat upright, nude.

He couldn't believe it. He wondered for a moment if it was all a terrible nightmare—the accident, the funeral, the last month of grieving. She looked to him and smiled, but there was something strange about her face. A few steps closer seemed to blur the image of her further.

"Kat?" His voice shook. "Tell me it's really you."

Each approaching step revealed what looked like a painting of his wife. As if one of the great renaissance painters came in the middle of the night to put her there for Gary to admire. But her eyes followed him. Her red lips stretched into a grin. *She was alive.*

Gary grabbed the flannel throw blanket from the edge of the sofa and tossed it over her chest. "You must be freezing."

She smelled of sugar-sweet vanilla. Her lips parted, strings of mucus between them—*no, not mucus*. Something else. Gary held a finger to the red stuff stretching between her lips. It was gritty between his fingers and smelled like frosting. He tasted the sugary icing and jumped back.

"Kat, can you talk to me?"

She stared at him, eyes desperate to communicate. He leaned in to listen but no words came from her mouth. Only the warm aroma of freshly baked cake escaped.

Heart thumping wildly against his chest, he paced the room, trying to figure out what to do next. She was back, and he had to keep her safe. "I've missed you." Gary wept, doubling over. "So much."

Slow as molasses, Kat leaned forward and raised from the chair. A thin layer of chocolate cake glued to flesh-colored icing remained on the seat. Gary ran to her, checking for damage. The entire layer of icing which formed her back was gone. The back of her legs and buttocks too were stripped of the frosting skin, exposing the porous dark cake beneath, divots and scars from where chunks had fallen off.

Gary held his palms out, unsure what to do to help her.

The flannel peeled away from her shoulders. Gravity tore it from her breasts, taking a slab of Kat with the blanket. It denuded her buttercream cover from her body and fell to the floor. Nothing remained of her breasts or belly. More nooks and crannies of her cakey insides were exposed.

Gary dove for the blanket, scraping her icing skin into his hands, then smeared it back on her body.

His gut lurched as he painted the crumble-filled frosting haphazardly onto Kat.

Her swirling icing eyes met with his. A gentle side to side of her head told him "no," but he couldn't lose her again. He scooped up all the bits he could and pressed them to her body. Clumps of cake flesh fell to the floor, so he pressed harder. His hand sank deep into her thigh where warm, moist cake slipped between his fingers. He retracted quickly, but the damage had been done. Kat's leg gave out and she collapsed to the floor. With no bones or muscles to support her, arms couldn't stop her fall. She smashed flat, arms diminishing to pieces upon impact. She lay with her face to the side, silently pleading.

He knelt beside her wrecked body. The perfect likeness of half a face was the only part left intact. He raised the back of his hand to wipe his tears, smearing cake and frosting across his cheek, nose, and lips.

He licked the sweet bits of dessert away. The delicate taste of his wife on his tongue calmed him. Gary closed his eyes, inserting a finger in his mouth, sucking the sweetness clean. Kat slid down his throat, into his belly. That bit of her would always be part of him.

But it wasn't enough. He needed more of her. He started with the crumbs. On hands and knees he crawled around scooping up her unsalvageable bits. Fistfuls of cake and icing went down his throat. When he finished with the floor, he went to work on the chair, licking it clean. Then the blanket. Bits of wooly flannel assaulted him as he scraped his teeth on the fabric. Belly distended, Gary pushed on until every bit of the mess surrounding Kat had been cleaned.

All that was left of Kat wasn't much to look at. A single leg and torso. One arm with an outstretched mangled hand. Her head, and the side of her gorgeous face.

Her expression begged him to stop, but he couldn't. The delectable taste of his wife was better than he'd ever imagined. Gary dove in for more. He reached for her hand which she tried to move, but her digits barely twitched. Digging fingers into spongy cake, he ripped her hand away from her arm and shoveled it into his mouth. Eating his way up her arm, to her shoulder, he came face to face with her. A saddened face begged him to stop...or maybe she begged him to get it over with.

Gary ran to the kitchen, slipping in frosting as he scrambled for a knife. He returned to her side and began to pet her black, glazed hair, his fingers leaving grooves in their wake.

He held the butcher's knife to the side of her face. "Happy anniversary, my love." The knife cut straight down in front of her ear, through her spongy head. Kat's face slivered off and landed in his hand. One last kiss to her red lips, and Gary devoured her—every crumb.

No matter how gravid and sick he became, he forced every last bit of his wife into his painful, swollen belly. Gary lay on the floor among the delectable viscera of his wife's remains, content that she would be part of him forever.

THE NORTH AMERICAN GUIDE TO ANIMAL SLAUGHTER

Nicole Wolverton

1.

Violet Nespoli removes the box from Miss Putterbaugh's freezer. She knows what will be inside, yet she gasps when she sees it: a single, perfect wedge of her late neighbor's almond cake.

"What's so great about old cake?" Nylah, her bestie since grade school, looks over her shoulder.

Violet shucks off her rubber gloves. "You don't understand. Miss Putterbaugh ate a slice every Sunday, warm and served with rum sauce. She'd never let anyone try it—said it was her own special treat."

"That's weird."

"Maybe. But it's almond cake, and I'm allergic to peanuts."

"So? Almonds aren't peanuts."

"To her, one nut allergy was the same as another," Violet says, "and she was sweet about it, like she was saving my life."

"Okay, well, trash it, and let's go."

"*Trash it*? Are you kidding? Now's my chance to finally try this cake."

"You can't be serious," Nylah says. "Do you want botulism? Because this is how you get botulism."

"Miss Putterbaugh's been dead for a week. The cake can't be much older than that, and it's frozen."

"You can still get botulism from frozen food."

"Miss Putterbaugh didn't die of botulism," Violet says. "She had a heart attack. And she left me her house, which means she wanted me to have everything in it. Like her last piece of cake."

Nylah makes a face. "And botulism. Or food poisoning, at least."

"Whatever." Violet transfers the cake to a plate and then to the microwave. The smell of stale air gives way to warm almonds. "Hand me a fork, please."

Violet takes her first bite. It's… light. No, it's *made* of light—she can feel warmth and recall the smell of the sunshine on grass. Every bite chases itself through her body.

"You going to lick the plate, too?" Nylah shakes her head. She sweeps the last Ziplocs full of mystery meat off the bottom shelf of the fridge and into the trash can. "There, done. So—how's your stomach?"

"I'm fine. You worry too much."

"You don't worry enough." Nylah closes the refrigerator door.

2.

It's rodeo day with the family. Violet sits in the stands and daydreams about Miss Putterbaugh's almond cake. She can think of nothing else.

Her mother nudges her knee. "Your brother's up next for the calf roping event."

Luke and his horse gallop out of the gate after the calf, but that's the last Violet pays any attention. Instead she thinks about finding that cake recipe. She's seen cookbooks in Miss Putterbaugh's house. They're everywhere—she even saw Miss Putterbaugh carry one into the backyard shed once.

Her mom and dad and clap. When it's over, Violet stands. "I'm going to walk around a little."

"Be careful, honey," her mom says. "You really should have dressed up a little—at least not worn all black. So off-putting and unladylike."

Violet walks down the bleachers to the food hall. Family outings suck. If it's not rodeo, it's 4H events, where Luke shows off the pigs that he and their father raise in a small pen in the backyard. Her stomach snarls. Maybe Nylah had been right about the cake, amazing as it was. Something isn't sitting right in there.

She turns down a corridor in search of the restroom. "Pardon me," Violet says to a guy in a rodeo badge, "where's the re—"

He smells like sunshine. That smell. It's coming from his neck, from the soft crease hiding his Adam's apple . Her mouth goes juicy. She wants to... take a bite. She skitters backward. But then there's a woman standing farther along, talking on her phone—the sunshine draws Violet forward. Maybe if she just licks the muscle in the woman's neck. That would be enough—wouldn't it? She gets within two feet of the woman before a voice screaming in her head tells her to stop. She storms away, shaking.

What's happening? She can practically feel her teeth sinking into tendons and arteries. Into meat and the fat. She stumbles into the women's restroom, and careens across the vestibule and into the row of stalls and sinks.

A moment later the door pushes open. In sweeps a woman wearing a top the color of a bull-fighter's cape. Her neck is long and slender. Swanlike. She turns to Violet. "What are you looking at, freak?"

The smell of her. It's delicious.

Violet springs up and takes a half-step towards her, then another, circling around the woman. That *smell*. Another half-step forward, circle around. It's a dance, and the woman doesn't know the steps. But Violet does.

The woman speaks, but Violet doesn't quite hear. She's focused on that long neck, on what she knows will be the finest skim of fat just beneath the skin. Violet's toes tense. Her stomach *wants*. She feels a surge of power and she hooks toward the woman, clamps down on her throat before the woman can make another sound. Then it's only her teeth and the crunch of the woman's throat and the hot meat.

Violet comes back to herself as though fighting to surface from the deepest sleep—the sunshine is everywhere. The floor is cold-warm. She pushes herself up and opens her eyes... and shrieks. She is head-to-toe blood. Gibbets of flesh stick to her cheek.

She trips backward, over something heavy. The woman's arms are splayed out, the inside of her throat exposed. Violet can still taste her: there are little strings of meat caught between her teeth. She digs at them with her tongue and leaps for the door to lock it out of pure instinct.

She squeaks a tender, terrified mewl and stares at the woman. Those dead eyes stare back. What has she done?

No amount of pacing brings a good plan to mind—or an explanation. There is only the light coursing through her, the sunshine on grass. Maybe Nylah was right—maybe it's botulism or food poisoning. A horrible strain. She focuses on the almond cake to keep herself from admitting that she's just killed a woman, from noticing the blood everywhere.

She's *killed* a *person*.

Violet holds in a shriek and does the only thing she can think to do: she calls Nylah.

3.

Violet does her best: she cleans herself up and rinses her clothes in a sink. It's lucky she's wearing black—it hides a multitude of sins. The woman—her name is Karen, something Violet discovers by rooting through her purse—continues to stare.

Violet scratches at her skin and paces. She texts her parents that she's not feeling well and went home. With every loop, she steps over Karen, carefully avoiding the pools of blood.

A knock sounds at the door, and Violet's phone buzzes at the same time. A text from Nylah: *I'm outside.*

She cracks open the door.

Nylah grins. "What's the emergency? And why are you drenched?"

"Did you bring the coat?" Violet slips out the door, locking it behind her.

Nylah unzips her bag and pulls out a long, dark trench. "What happened?"

"I dropped pizza down my shirt." Violet slips into the coat, relief like a flood. At least for a few seconds. She might be able to get out of the arena, but the fact remains: she *ate* a human being.

During the drive home, Violet barely hears anything Nylah says—she thinks about the cake, about the blood. "Can you drop me at Miss Putterbaugh's house instead?" Violet says. "I think there might have been something wrong with that cake I ate."

"I told you. Let me guess—you didn't spill anything. You puked all over yourself, right?"

"Is that what happens when you get botulism?"

"No, food poisoning."

"Ever heard of craving meat—or maybe fat—as a symptom of eating spoiled food?" Violet asks.

"What, like big, fatty steak?"

"Yeah, sure. Steak."

"Uh uh. But my mom had something like that, though," Nylah says. "It was a nutritional deficiency. Like low iron or protein."

"Did your mom ever say that she wanted to... bite someone?"

"No, but—wait, is this a sex thing? Because I dreamed I bit that junior on the golf team once, and that was definitely a sex thing. Or . . . are you pregnant? People crave all sorts of weird stuff with they're pregnant."

"I hadn't thought about that." Violet folds her arms over her stomach. The prom with Mike, the guy from bio class. It's possible.

"Oh, shit. Should we stop at a drug store and pick up a pregnancy test?"

Violet's stomach gurgles. "Would you drop me at Miss Putterbaugh's first? I'll give you a twenty to go pick one up for me." She closes her eyes and dreams of the smell of sunshine on grass.

4.

Violet can't stop shivering, even after showering off the rest of the blood in Miss Putterbaugh's bathroom. Even after exchanging her blood-stained clothes for something clean. Even after her mother calls to say the police have sequestered the crowd inside the arena for questioning, but no one understands why. Violet thinks of Karen's staring eyes. Of the blood.

She touches her stomach.

The cake could be coincidence. She did feel a flutter in her stomach when she ate it—fetuses do that. The prom was only a month ago—do month-old fetuses cause flutters? Google tells her no. The fetus is only the size of a poppy seed. A murderous poppy seed.

Poppy seeds are in cake sometimes.

Violet really wants more cake.

She starts with the cookbooks in the living room. She wants the smell of light back, chasing itself through her veins. She searches the house and comes up with nothing. There's only one place left she can think to look: the backyard shed.

Violet edges through the shed door and flicks the light switch. The inside of the shed is sparkling clean, with a wooden table against the back wall that stretches from one side of the shed to the other. Several saws hang from pegboard mounted next to the table, and on the edge lies a thick book with a yellow cover. The title: *The North American Guide to Animal Slaughter.*

She takes the book with her back inside the house to wait for Nylah. She perches on the couch and flips through the book.

Each chapter illustrates the proper way to slaughter a different animal and cut it into parts. Cows. Sheep. The photos are bloody, as bad as the women's room. Toward the back, Miss Putterbaugh's spiky handwriting marks the chapter on pigs.

Luke and her father talk pigs constantly, but the only thing Violet knows is that pig anatomy is similar to human anatomy. Miss Putterbaugh's handwriting labels exactly what's different in humans. Karen's eyes seem to stare up at her from the page.

Paperclipped to the next page is a single piece of paper with a list of names and dates. Violet digs out her phone and searches the first name on the list. Charles Vessy III. Missing for thirty years. Next is Bernard Abernathy. His blood-covered car was found twenty-five years ago, but not him. It goes on, name after name. Missing, presumed dead. Sometimes suspicion of foul play.

Karen's voice whispers in Violet's head: *Think. Make the connection, you freak.*

Violet refuses.

It's the poppy seed. It's the hormones.

She turns the page. Written in the margin, is the recipe for Miss Putterbaugh's almond cake. There, third line down: one cup of mincemeat made from suet.

Human suet.

She heaves the book away from her and tries to make herself small. So small that she cannot remember the name of the woman she murdered—the woman she ate. So small that she cannot remember the taste of the cake. So small that she cannot hear the front door when it opens.

But suddenly Nylah is there, and her lips are moving, saying words that Violet cannot hear. Not when Nylah smells so amazing, like sunshine on grass. Violet surges off the couch. She takes a half-step forward, then another, circling around Nylah. Another half-step forward, circle around. It's a dance, and Nylah doesn't know the steps.

But Violet does.

MRS BETTY BRIGGS AND THE ANGEL FOOD CAKE FROM HELL

Kelly Robinson

When Betty Briggs won the blue ribbon in cake baking at the 1957 Franklinville Fair, the women rallied around to congratulate her. Even Dotty-Jean Driskell, who everyone thought was a sure win with her Coconut Double Delight, hosted a celebratory tea the next Sunday after church. They all agreed that although Betty had made a simple angel food cake, it was certainly a fine one.

The next year, when Betty won again with the exact same cake, the reception was less enthusiastic. Dotty-Jean took second with her Plum Perfect Chiffon, and Loretta Sykes was third with her Daffy Daffodil Cake, filled with a surprise banana curd instead of the usual lemon. Anyone sharp-eyed would have spotted Dotty-Jean and Loretta exchanging a look when Mayor Hurley pinned the blue ribbon on Betty for the second time. A photographer took Betty's picture for the *Daily Onlooker.* No one hosted a tea.

They might not have been so envious if Betty had won any other competition twice in a row. Why, old Mrs. Jarvis had been sweeping the sweet pickle category since before anybody could remember. The cake competition was different, because it was sponsored by Daisy Flour. The best cake at the fair not only received $100 in cash, but the winner's name and face were featured on the Daisy store display at the A&P. Winning best cake was like being the Queen of Franklinville.

It didn't take a sharp eye to notice the women's strained smiles when Betty Briggs won again in '59, '60, and '61. They had exhausted themselves trying to beat her, their cakes increasing in layers year by year, becoming towering confections studded with fresh berries and hand-whipped cream, or, in the case of Dotty-Jean's most deeply-devastating second place win, wrapped in vines of marzipan ivy. Maddy Simmons had now made so many test versions of her Double Dutch Chocolate Dream that the twins, Todd and Terry, were bursting out of their school clothes.

Something had to be done. That's what Dotty-Jean said to her husband when the contest loomed once again, as she dried the dishes one Sunday afternoon.

"Something has to be done."

"What's that, dear?" Hal monotoned from behind his *Onlooker.*

"I'm talking about Betty Briggs. Winning every year with the same old angel food cake!"

"Maybe she made a deal with the Devil," Hal said, and then chuckled. As was his habit when he said something he thought was particularly funny, he said it again, as if he had a big audience and wanted to make sure no one missed it.

Dotty-Jean ignored him. She dried her hands and took off her apron. It was her favorite, sheer white dotted swiss with a patch pocket shaped like a heart, but today it brought her no joy. Her mouth was a straight line.

After dinner, she called an emergency meeting. Dotty-Jean served hot coffee with a splash of Sambuca and they got down to business. The bake-off was only two weeks away, and they all agreed: a sixth win from Betty Briggs would be unacceptable.

"It's absurd" said Loretta Sykes. "It's like having the same Miss America over and over."

Maddy Simmons said she'd heard a rumor that Betty had been canning, and might enter her bread-and-butter pickles this year, too.

Lois Finney was aghast. "If she wins sweet pickles, why Mrs. Jarvis might just as well lay down and die."

Dotty-Jean suggested that the judges might be crooked, but they dismissed it. They all believed in the integrity of Daisy Flour. It said right on the label: *The brand you can trust.*

Sarah Snell, who never spoke much, piped up from the corner love seat.

"The thing is," Sarah said, "Betty's cake is really good." The room was hushed for a moment, but they recognized it as the truth. Dotty-Jean had to agree.

"It *is* good" she admitted.

Maddy chimed in that it didn't even make sense for a plain old angel food cake to taste so good, but it did.

"And yet," she said, rolling her eyes, "She swears there's no secret ingredient."

Before they disbanded, they'd had more Sambuca than any of them meant to have, and they made a plan to find out Betty's secret.

Dotty-Jean grilled the neighborhood grocer, Mr. Levin, but he'd never seen her buy anything more unusual than a bag of salt. Maddy scoured the library for angel food cake recipes, but found nothing useful. Lois Finney, who had just read the *Reader's Digest* condensed version of *Stopover: Tokyo* and was all hyped up on secret agents, tailed Betty all the way to the big A&P. She moved boxes of cream of wheat to spy on Betty in the baking goods, next to her very own picture on the Daisy display. She didn't buy anything special, but Lois overheard her tell a clerk she was baking her practice cake next Wednesday night.

The next morning, while Dotty-Jean was still having her coffee and thinking about vacuuming the curtains, Loretta Sykes barged in.

"Call the girls," she said. "Tell them I've got something huge. Huge!"

When they were all assembled, Loretta spoke breathlessly.

"I stopped by the Briggs' this morning, thinking I could chat with Betty over coffee, maybe get something out of her."

"What did she say?" asked Maddy.

"Nothing! I knocked and there was no answer, so I went inside and called out. That's when I heard the vacuum upstairs. She couldn't hear me."

"Cut to the chase," barked Lois.

"I looked around for the secret ingredient, but then I saw *this* next to the toaster."

Loretta pulled it out of her purse and held it up like it was the Holy Grail.

"I stole her recipe box."

They erupted into so many whoops it sounded like the kids when they played Custer's Last Stand.

Loretta thrust the box at Dotty-Jean, who sat down while the others crowded around. There were dozens of index cards, all neatly typed by Betty on her husband's Remington

Quiet-riter. She read out the names as she flipped through each recipe.

"Lemon icebox pie. Toll House cookies. Banana pudding. Angel food ... here it is!" Her eyes scanned the card.

"Read it!" they all cried.

"I ... I can't. I don't know what this is." She turned it over.

Lois snatched it from her. "I'll read it."

"Be my guest," said Dotty-Jean.

Lois stared. "What on God's earth ...?"

It was handwritten with heavy black ink, in what might be Latin. The card itself was older than the rest, brittle and brown with age. The reverse side was covered with drawings, mostly circles intersected with lines and weird symbols.

"Is that how you're supposed to cut the cake?" asked Maddy.

"It's not anything," said Lois. "It's a joke. She planted that nonsense there so she could laugh at us."

There was only one plan left: they would spy on Betty Briggs while she made her practice cake. If there were any secret method to her baking, they would have to see it with their own eyes.

Wednesday night, they all met up, dressed in their darkest navy slacks and cardigans. The plan wouldn't even be possible if the Briggs' house weren't situated the way it was, with a high row of shrubs lining the kitchen side of the house. The neighbors couldn't see in, but in the small space between the shrubbery and the window, there was a clear view right into the kitchen—and the dining area beyond.

They crowded together.

"Why did she move the furniture?" whispered Lois.

"Maybe she waxed the floor," said Maddy.
"It *does* look really good," said Loretta.
"Shhhhhhhh," said Dotty-Jean.
They watched as Betty Briggs cracked and separated several eggs. She sifted the flour. ("I usually sift *twice*," sneered Lois.) Betty picked up a huge container of salt.
"That's a lot of salt," said Dotty-Jean.
Betty moved to the dining room area. As the women watched agape, she poured the salt on the floor, making a big circle.
Lois gasped.
"I can't see! What did she do?" said Loretta.
"She just poured a bunch of salt on the floor!" said Lois.
Betty returned to the kitchen and took something out of a bag, but they couldn't see what it was. Then Betty unbuttoned her blouse.
"Maybe it's hot?" said Loretta.
Betty slipped out of her skirt next, and then began to remove her undergarments. Soon she was standing in her kitchen completely naked. The women were transfixed by Betty's naked body moving around the kitchen as though it were normal. She retrieved the item that had been in the bag, which they now saw was a dead, unplucked chicken.
"I don't like this," said Sarah.
Betty placed the chicken on a cutting board, chopped off its head in one swift movement and then held it up, letting its blood trickle all over her breasts, then she rubbed the creature all over herself, smearing the blood around until her torso was

covered. She took the ingredients into the dining room and placed them in the circle: the sifted flour, the beaten egg whites, the sugar and vanilla.

Betty chanted some words they couldn't hear, but as her voice rose, they caught bits of it.

"It's the words from the card," whispered Loretta.

Betty lay down in the center of the circle with her arms and legs spread out wide, as if she were about to make a snow angel. What happened next defied logic, but it seemed as if the floor of the dining room dissolved before their eyes and became earth. From the dark loam, a tremendous tentacle wormed its way up, and then several smaller ones pushed through, like the time-lapse films of sprouting plants they saw on the Disney nature shows.

Lois screamed, but it didn't matter. Betty's eyes rolled up as she lolled on the floor. The tentacles writhed around her and surrounded her body, while the largest one snaked up her leg and then entered her. The smallest tentacles wrapped around her arms as others undulated into her orifices until she and the squiggling arms of pulsating flesh were like one massive creature. They moved in and out of her in unison, and the ones that weren't inside of her rose up and waved about like seaweed underwater, before curling back up on themselves.

When the tentacles withdrew, they made a seeping, sucking sound so loud the women outside could hear it. The creatures (or creature, as it was hard to tell if it was many things, or parts of one enormous thing) slid back into the earth. Betty Briggs was lying on the floor, which they noticed was now a floor again. They wondered if what they'd seen had actually happened, but seeing Betty, now covered with a thick slime as well as the chicken blood, they knew it had.

Loretta Sykes threw up in the azaleas. The other women attended to her, then decided they had seen enough and should go home. Dotty-Jean went back for a last look inside and saw Betty Briggs, clean and dressed, pouring batter into a pan.

Betty Briggs' angel food cake won the blue ribbon at the fair that year. None of the women thought it was strange. What *was* strange was that the next year at bake-off time, Levin's grocery sold out of salt. Even stranger was that around the same time, the butcher shop had an unusual number of requests for whole, unprocessed chickens.

But strangest *of all* was the fact that at the 1963 Franklinville Fair, the Daisy Flour cake bake-off was declared an unprecedented six-way tie.

Hal Driskell nudged the fellow next to him at the award ceremony and said, "I guess they all made a deal with the Devil this year." And in case the man didn't catch it, he said it again. The men both laughed and laughed, the women on the stage beamed like beauty pageant winners, and down below the surface of the ground on which they stood, something old and sinister twisted in the earth.

THE RITUAL

Benjamin Franke

The weight of the knife is eclipsed only by the heaviness that comes with this day. I inspect the instrument in my hand. The cold steel is long and looks to be razor sharp. There is an echo of its chill on my palm as it moves around in my hand absorbing some of my heat into it.

This blade seems excessive, but it is the one that ceremony dictates for the approaching ritual, so it is the one I will use. I think about testing the edge with my thumb, but it is not me that this blade will taste tonight. Instead, I set it beside the offering laying prepared on our makeshift altar.

The lights dim, leaving the room aglow from candles that have been positioned with great care. The members, who have gathered as witnesses, begin chanting in the unpracticed rhythmic tone that comes from infrequent gatherings. This does not matter, nor do they falter in their role because of it. The melody of the incantation is not important. No, it is the words; words that must be repeated four times, bringing my own title into the rite. On cue, as the last line finishes resonating through the chamber, the flickering flames go out in unison. This is a good omen.

I return the knife to my hand as one of the members returns light to this small room. I hover over the offering, not sure exactly where to plunge the weapon first. It is always different and decided upon in the moment. While making my decision, I admire the symbols and icons that adorn the body. I try to find a path that will allow me maximum impact while preserving the age-old art, even if for only a few moments.

A path decided, I plunge the knife deep, passing easily through the layers until the tip is obstructed and can penetrate no further. I push down against the curve of the blade and ease it out as I do so. The blade is stained crimson. This excites me – this excites everyone, even though it was expected. It is hard to contain our eagerness and some members have begun stirring.

The ritual is almost complete. I pierce, cut, and slash leaving bits of matter behind as I cast odd sized chunks about the room. No longer am I concerned with tradition or ceremony, just the completion of the task set before me.

I pick up a piece that I managed to hold back for just this moment. I bite deeply. The thick red substance that I have longed for since it first revealed itself during the ritual spills from my mouth and hangs at the corner of my lip threatening to be lost among my graying beard. I lap it up, refusing to allow any of this offering to go to waste.

And now that my task is complete, now that the birthday ritual is finished and the cake is no more, I must accept the weight brought on by this day - down the hill I go.

About the Authors

V CASTRO is a Mexican American woman originally from Texas, now residing in the UK. You can find out more about her books on her website vvcastro.com. Her most recent stories include, The Cucuy of Cancun in *Worst Laid Plans* and Templo Mayor in *Graveyard Smash* from Kandisha Press. Tres Leches is a story set in the same universe as The Cucuy of Cancun, as V expands the mythology of the creatures in her stories.

E. SENECA is a freelance speculative fiction author with a strong affinity for horror and dark fantasy. Some of her works include Harvesters, published in Grimmer & Grimmer Books' anthology *DeadSteam*, It Lives in the Mineshaft, A Specific Sort of Shared Madness, and Haunt Me Like a Memory, published by Soteira Press in their *Monsters* anthology series. She has written original fiction since 2008, and can be found on Twitter @esenecaauthor.

STEPHANIE YU is a writer of speculative fiction. She lives in Los Angeles with her partner Nate. Her work has previously appeared in *Eclectica* and was a finalist in *CRAFT*'s 2019 Flash Fiction Contest. You can find her on Twitter @stfu_stephanie

DOUGLAS FORD lives and works on the west coast of Florida, just off an exit made famous by a Jack Ketchum short story. His weird and dark fiction has appeared in *Dark Moon Digest*, *Infernal Ink* and *Weird City*, along with several other small press publications. Recent work has appeared in *The Best Hardcore Horror Volumes Three and Four*, and a novella, *The Reattachment*, appeared in 2019 courtesy of Madness Heart Press. Upcoming publications include a collection of short fiction from Madness Heart Press and stories set to appear in *Diabolical Plots* and *The Half You See*.

TIFFANY MICHELLE BROWN ran away from the scorching deserts of Arizona to live near breezy California beaches. Despite a sunny disposition, she's inspired by dark, stormy nights and once had a heart-to-heart with a ghost over a beer. Tiffany's work has been featured by the NoSleep Podcast, Trembling with Fear, Sirens Call Publications, Camden Park Press and Hellbound Books.

SAM RICHARD is the owner of Weirdpunk Books, and co-editor of the Splatterpunk Award-nominated *The New Flesh: A Literary Tribute to David Cronenberg* and editor of *Zombie Punks Fuck Off*. He is the author of the short-story collection, *To Wallow in Ash & Other Sorrows*, the novella, *Sabbath of the Fox-Devils*, and his short fiction has appeared in *Oculus Sinister*, *LAZERMALL*, *Breaking Bizarro*, and many other anthologies and magazines. Widowed in 2017, he slowly rots in Minneapolis, MN with his dog Nero.

JACKSON NASH is a British author. In 2020 he was shortlisted for the Creative Future Writer's Award and is a fellow of the Lambda Literary Foundation Writer's Retreat for Emerging LGBTQ+ Voices. Recently his poetry has appeared in *TypeHouse Literary Magazine* and *Impossible Archetype.* Jackson identifies as a queer trans man (he/him).

R.J. JOSEPH earned her MFA in Writing Popular Fiction from Seton Hill University and currently works as an associate professor of English. She's had several stories published in various venues, including two anthologies of horror written by black female writers, *Sycorax's Daughters* and *Black Magic Women* as well as in *Road Kill: Texas Horror from Texas Writers, Vol. 2*, a volume of horror by Texas horror writers. Her academic essays have also appeared in applauded collections, such as the Stoker award finalist *Uncovering Stranger Things: Essays on Eighties Nostalgia, Cynicism and Innocence in the Series.* Her most recent essay appears in the collection *The Streaming of Hill House: Essays on the Haunting Netflix Series.*

RISA WOLF is a nonbinary writer who currently lives in the Philadelphia PA area. When not haunting libraries and taking photos of herons, they write in their blog at killerpuppytails.com

LIAM HOGAN is an award winning short story writer, with stories in *Best of British Science Fiction 2016 & 2019*, and *Best of British Fantasy 2018* (NewCon Press). He's been published by *Analog*, Daily Science Fiction, and Flame Tree Press, among others. He helps host Liars' League London, volunteers at the creative writing charity Ministry of Stories, and lives and avoids work in London. More details at happyendingnotguaranteed.blogspot.co.uk

BELINDA FERGUSON has pursued careers as a pastry chef, a belly dancer and a health care administrator. She has been telling stories most of her life. Currently she lives in Halifax, Nova Scotia with her husband Steve, and a black cat called Kismet. One of whom is her very best friend, but she will not say which one.

MADISON MCSWEENEY is a Canadian poet and horror author. She has published tales of fantasy and the macabre in outlets like *American Gothic, Unnerving Magazine,* and *Zombie Punks Fuck Off,* and her poetry has appeared in *Cockroach Conservatory* and the *Twin Peaks* anthology *These Poems Are Not What They Seem.* She also blogs (mostly about rock music and genre fiction) at madisonmcsweeney.com

RED LAGOE enjoys spewing her love of the macabre onto the page every chance she gets, after being raised on 80s horror.

Her fiction collection, *Lucid Screams* was released in February 2020, and several of her short stories have been published by Crystal Lake Publishing, *Dark Moon Digest*, Sinister Smile Press and more.

NICOLE WOLVERTON is a Philadelphia-based writer of adult and young adult fiction. Her short stories have appeared in *Aji* magazine, Jersey Devil Press, The Molotov Cocktail, and elsewhere, as well as in several anthologies, including the *Coffin Blossoms* anthology (Jolly Horror Press) and the upcoming *Imaginary Friends: The Half That You See* anthology (Dark Ink Books). Her adult psychological thriller, *The Trajectory of Dreams*, was published by Bitingduck Press. You can find her online at nicolewolverton.com and on Twitter @nicolewolverton.

KELLY ROBINSON is a Bram Stoker Award-nominated writer and a contributor to horror magazines like *Scary Monsters* and *Rue Morgue*. She is a recipient of the Horror Writers Association's Rocky Wood Memorial Scholarship for Non-Fiction Writing, and is the founder, host, and curator of Knoxferatu, a silent horror film festival in Knoxville, Tennessee.

BENJAMIN FRANKE lives in the snow-belt of central New York where he works as a regional truck driver. A lover of stories with much time on his hands, Ben spends his time on the road thinking of new tales to share with fellow readers.

TRIGGER WARNINGS

Naturally, horror often involves troubling themes, but we're conscious that some of our stories might not be quite what you're expecting from a cake-based anthology.

The following list isn't exhaustive, but it takes into account certain themes and situations included in *Slashertorte*:

- Abuse (emotional/psychological)
- Anxiety/depression
- Loss of a partner
- Pregnancy/miscarriage
- Torture

Also, you may find several stories worrying if you're concerned by eating disorders, although none are mentioned by name.